I LOVE HOW YOU LOVE ME

The Sullivans

Bella Andre

I LOVE HOW YOU LOVE ME
~ The Sullivans ~
Dylan & Grace
© 2014 Bella Andre

Dylan Sullivan, a renowned boat builder, has spent his entire life sailing around the world. But while he's always enjoyed the freedom of the ocean, when Grace Adrian shows up at his Seattle boathouse to interview him for a magazine, it's love at first sight. Love for both Grace and her ten-month-old son, Mason, with whom Dylan has an immediate bond. And every moment they spend together makes Dylan more and more certain that a love like theirs is worth risking everything for.

A year and a half ago, Grace's entire world turned upside down. Not only did she learn that she was pregnant, she also found out that she was nothing but a dirty little secret to her boyfriend and his elite Washington, D.C., family. Since then, Grace has been rebuilding her life in Seattle, giving one hundred percent of her attention to her son and her freelance writing career. Believing she can never risk her heart—or her son's—again, especially to a man like Dylan who could sail away at any moment, Grace tries desperately to guard her heart from the charismatic and sexy sailor.

For as sweet and protective as Dylan is during the day, at night when one incredibly hot kiss turns into so much more, Grace simply can't find a way to stop herself from tumbling into his arms. But can she ever learn to trust in love again?

A note from Bella:

After writing more than a dozen stories about the Sullivan family, I'm not only more in love with them than ever, I'm also amazed by the way each of them surprises me while I'm writing his or her story. After I finished writing the draft of *I Love How You Love Me* and began rereading it to polish it up for publication, I realized that somewhere along the way Dylan Sullivan had risen in the ranks to become one of my new favorite heroes.

It's love at first sight for him when he first meets Grace Adrian and her ten-month-old son...and boy, does he show her how much he adores her over and over and over throughout the book. I love heroes like him—sweet and protective, but also *so* incredibly sexy. I hope you fall just as hard for Dylan, Grace, and little Mason as I have!

If this is your first time reading about the Sullivans, you can easily read each book as a stand-alone—and there is a Sullivan family tree available on my website (http://bellaandre.com/wp-content/uploads/2014/02/SullivanFamilyTree.pdf)
so you can see how the books connect together.

Happy reading,
Bella Andre

CHAPTER ONE

Grace Adrian needed Dylan Sullivan. Badly enough that when the babysitter she'd scheduled to watch her ten-month-old son bailed on her at the last second, she strapped Mason into the backseat of her car and headed down to the Seattle harbor with him.

Fifteen minutes later, she pulled into the parking lot beside Dylan's boathouse. Mason, who had been happily gnawing on his favorite stuffed giraffe during the drive, immediately lifted his arms to her when she opened the rear door.

"I've got to unstrap you first, cutie." The second he was free, he all but jumped into her arms. She closed her eyes as she caught him and cuddled him close. The past year and a half hadn't been easy, but she wouldn't trade her son, or her immense love for him, for anything.

Grace had plenty of regrets...but Mason wasn't one of them.

She was just shifting him to her hip so that she could straighten out her navy-blue suit when he whimpered. "Do you want to take your giraffe with you?" She handed it to him, but he batted it out of her hand. "We'll have to clean him before you put him back in your mouth," she said in a gentle voice as she picked up the stuffed toy from the ground and put it into the car, "but don't worry, I have another one of your favorite toys." Mason immediately began to shake the multicolored circular rattle she handed him.

Grace did her best to adjust her clothes, then ran a hand through her long, dark hair in an effort to look as professional as possible while she spoke with Dylan. At least, she hoped she was going to speak to him today, given that he hadn't returned a single one of her phone messages over the past week. She would have sent him an email if she could have found a website or email address for him, but he was one of the few people on the planet who didn't seem to have either. Which was, she'd decided, just plain weird. How did he run his business if people couldn't reach him?

"Time to go track down the elusive Mr. Sullivan," she said to Mason as they headed together across the parking lot.

Her son bore down hard with his gums on his toy by way of response, but it was good enough for Grace. She'd become a master at one-sided conversations during the past ten months, and it was amazing just how much she could find to say on her end, even when the only response she ever got was a gurgle, giggle, or wail.

"Let's pray that he's nice and willing to cooperate."

The strange thing was how little information she'd been able to find about Dylan. No interviews, nothing where he was talking himself up. What kind of man didn't want to promote himself? Especially when he was not only one of the most respected wooden-sailboat makers on the West Coast, and a multi-winning sailboat racer, but he was also related to some of the wealthiest—and most well-known—people in the world, including a movie star, two rock stars, and a billionaire CEO.

It was only one of the many questions she needed to ask him.

But while she hadn't been able to find much written information about him on the Internet, she'd found plenty of pictures. Grace had vowed never to be wowed by a pretty face ever again, but that didn't mean she didn't notice a good-looking guy when she saw one. And there was no doubt whatsoever that Dylan was a very attractive man.

Still, she couldn't help but think he'd be a heck of a lot more attractive if he actually returned one of her phone calls.

As she carefully dodged one of the puddles from the previous evening's rainstorm and breathed in the sweet yet salty sea air on the surprisingly warm and muggy day, she thought again how happy she was about her move to Seattle. Sure, it rained quite a bit, but she loved how dust never had a chance to settle. Plus, constant rain meant there was water pretty much everywhere. She'd grown up on a farm half an hour outside of Washington, D.C., and had loved playing in the river and streams, but the only time she'd been out on the ocean had been with her ex a year and a half ago. She'd loved the sea breeze and the feel of the water rushing beneath the sailboat. Unfortunately, the sail had barely lasted fifteen minutes because her ex had gotten green around the gills and ordered the captain to take them back to shore.

A seagull swooping toward the water just a few feet in front of them brought her back to the present. Mason dropped his toy to point at it excitedly and she agreed, "It is very exciting!" even though the gull came up empty-beaked. But when Mason looked down at his hand a few seconds later and realized his toy was gone, his face crumpled.

Uh-oh. The last thing she needed was to be holding a crying baby when she finally met Dylan.

Grace quickly bent down, and her pre-baby suit skirt tightened even more around her hips as she picked up the rattle. Normally she would never give the toy back to Mason without washing it thoroughly first, but when he started to cry, she simply tried her best to shake off the dirt before he shoved it back into his mouth. She reminded herself that she'd eaten plenty of dirt growing up on a farm and had lived through it just fine.

Not, unfortunately, that the toy seemed to be making any difference as Mason let loose with a loud wail, then chucked the plastic rattle so that it landed with a loud bang on the wooden dock.

"Mason, sweetie, don't cry. Please don't cry." She brushed a hand over his hair, then across his wet cheeks. "We just need to spend a few minutes here and then we'll get you home for your nap." But the more she tried to soothe him, the more Mason fussed in her arms.

"Everything okay out there?"

She looked up at the dark-haired man who had stepped out of the boathouse...and literally lost her breath. Dylan Sullivan was a million times better looking in person than he'd been online. And he'd been pretty amazing looking on her computer screen.

She'd wondered what a boat builder's uniform was, and now she knew: T-shirt, worn blue jeans, and heavy work boots. The dark hair beneath his ball cap was a little too long and just unruly enough to make a girl want to drop everything to run her hands through it. But given that she had taught herself to be fairly immune to good-looking men, his movie-star looks alone wouldn't have been enough to send her breath whooshing from her lungs.

It was the concern in his eyes as he took in Mason's distress that completely undid her.

"Everything is fine, thanks."

Mason turned to look up at her, then, and even though he couldn't yet speak, she could clearly read his mind. *I am not fine!* Her son followed up his silent message with a far less silent one that echoed off the surface of the water in a shockingly loud way.

"Mason, sweet boy, everything's okay," she said again as she rocked and murmured, kissed and bounced, trying anything she could to shift him out of his crying jag. Dylan had walked several paces closer by this time, which only made her more flustered. "I just fed him before we came here, so he shouldn't be hungry. And," she added as she gave Mason a soft pat on his bottom to check the state of his diaper, "he's dry and clean."

"Does he want his toy back?"

She hadn't noticed Dylan picking up the plastic rattle from the dock. When he held it out, she realized she'd never seen a man like him— so big and rugged and over-the-top gorgeous— holding a baby toy before. It did funny things to her stomach, sending it into flips and spins.

Miraculously, Mason stopped crying as he looked at Dylan. And then, suddenly, her son twisted in her arms and reached out. She assumed he was trying to grab the toy, but when he batted it away again, it became clear that he was really reaching for Dylan.

Her heart stopped in her chest. Actually just quit beating for a moment. Mason had never reached for anyone but her. But one look at this beautiful stranger and he was instinctively reaching out to be held?

Must run in our family.

Wait. No. That was crazy. She didn't want to reach for Dylan. Didn't want the gorgeous sailboat maker to pull her into his arms, hold her, and never let go. She was just tired and stressed and overwhelmed because she hadn't had anyone else to lean on in so long.

Plus, it didn't help that just that morning she'd read an article online about her ex—a high-profile man from D.C.—having fertility problems with his wife. Because now Grace was more desperate than ever for Dylan's cooperation with the magazine story she was hoping to write about him.

It had been a year and a half since she'd made her initial pitch to *Sailing Magazine* about a piece on the heart of a sailor, inspired by her first and only sail. She hadn't yet realized she was pregnant, and she hadn't been dumped yet, either. Her pitch had been good enough that the editor had actually seemed upset when he'd told her they didn't have the budget for the story. Fast forward to a week ago, when she'd been beyond shocked to see the email from the magazine's editor-in-chief telling her they hadn't been able to stop thinking about her story idea and had finally pulled together the budget for it. The money they had offered her for the article, along with the promise that it would be a cover story, had blown her mind. Both couldn't have come at a better time, considering how little there was in her bank account now that she lived in such an expensive part of the country. She couldn't believe her luck—at least until the editor had told her his one big requirement for the story: Dylan Sullivan had to agree not only to be the main subject...but the cover boy as well.

If he didn't agree to the interview, the editor would pull the story that would not only pay the next few months' rent, but would also increase her legal defense fund so that she could hire a really good custody lawyer if her ex ever decided to try to take Mason away from her.

"Would it help if I held him for a little while?"

Dylan's softly spoken question broke her out of her spinning thoughts. She'd never given her child to a stranger to hold, wouldn't have thought she would ever consider it. "Maybe if you could just hold his hand for a few seconds, that will be enough to calm him down a little."

"Hey there, big boy." Dylan stroked Mason's fingers. "Welcome to my boathouse."

But her son not only kept crying, he was leaning so close to Dylan by then that he had practically wriggled all the way out of her arms.

From the look on Mason's face, along with the tenor of his wails, Grace knew they were approximately five seconds from an even more massive meltdown. Which was why, at last, Grace made the only decision she felt she could to try to keep her son from more misery: She let him go into the arms of the man by whom he so badly wanted to be held.

Dylan took him with the ease of a man who had held plenty of babies. And who liked holding them. To her further amazement, by the time he said, "What's your name?" to her son, Mason had stopped crying and was babbling a greeting in his own special language.

"Mason," Grace replied. "His name is Mason." And her little boy was smiling now, so happy that his entire face had lit up. "He's never wanted to go to anyone else like this before."

Dylan shifted his gaze to her, and she felt as though his dark brown eyes saw all the way down into her soul. When her son grunted to get his attention, he turned to grin back down at him.

"You've got quite a throwing arm, haven't you, Mason?" As if to confirm it, the baby grabbed the baseball cap off Dylan's head and sent it sailing into the air.

Grace hurried to pick up Dylan's hat before the breeze took it into the water. "Mason is usually pretty mellow. I think maybe the muggy heat is getting to him."

Or perhaps that was just her, because every time Dylan looked at her she felt as if she were heating up from the inside out. Which was crazy on a number of fronts. First, for the past year and a half she'd been completely shut down when it came to men. Second, she was here for professional, not personal, reasons. And third, the chance of ever moving beyond *professional* with a man like Dylan Sullivan was utterly laughable.

But when she handed him his hat, the stark heat in his gaze nearly had her dropping it from suddenly numb fingertips. Fumbling, she ended up shoving the cap at him.

"I can take my son back now." But when she reached for Mason, he only snuggled closer into Dylan's broad chest.

"I'm okay holding him for a while longer if you're okay with it," Dylan offered.

God, no, she wasn't okay with it for a whole host of twisted-together reasons. It wasn't just that Mason had chosen a stranger instead of her for the first time. It was more that she thought she'd made her peace with her son never knowing his father—only now that she'd seen Mason in a man's arms, it was hitting her all over again, harder than ever, that he'd never have this. At least, not for more than these few minutes with Dylan.

Standing in front of a stranger from whom she desperately needed help—one who was holding her son so sweetly—Grace couldn't figure out how to stop her heart from breaking into a million pieces all over again.

Or to keep from falling head over heels for Dylan the same way it seemed her son just had.

CHAPTER TWO

Two years ago, Dylan had been sailing in Belize when he'd looked up and seen a rogue wave come crashing toward him and his boat. He hadn't stopped to think, hadn't had time to be afraid, had simply done whatever he could to sail through what was later called the "storm of the century." And he'd known that every second he'd spent in a sailboat during the past two decades had been to prepare him for that moment.

Seeing Grace and Mason for the first time had felt exactly the same way. He'd been working in his boathouse, enjoying the quiet and the physical labor, when he'd heard crying, and then the somewhat desperate murmur of a woman's voice as she tried to calm the baby. The moment he'd stepped outside to make sure neither of them were hurt, and set eyes on the mother and child, his entire world had spun off its axis.

Desire for the woman—and his need to soothe the little boy—had come so fast that he hadn't stopped to overthink or be afraid of what he was feeling. He'd simply reached out for the baby at the same time that he'd confirmed the little boy's mother wasn't wearing a wedding ring...and thought, *I'm going to marry her.*

Maybe he should have been surprised, but he wasn't. Not when he'd always known that this would be how he'd love. All or nothing. And faster than a sloop flying over the water at twenty-five knots. All the years he'd spent watching his parents together, along with the way his cousins and siblings had found love these past few years, had prepared him well for this moment when he'd be hit by his own lightning bolt straight to the heart.

Dylan had never second-guessed himself. He'd always known he would be a sailor and build boats. There had been small struggles along the way, of course, but he'd never doubted his direction or his beliefs. So when he'd stepped close to Grace and the sparks between them practically exploded from nothing more than that, he'd barely been able to keep from sealing both their fates with a kiss.

But he hadn't been raised to be an idiot. Which was why he wasn't going to let himself pull her closer and kiss her.

Not yet, anyway.

"I have some cold drinks inside the boathouse. If you have a few minutes, why don't you come in and have one?"

"Thank you," she said as she gave him a small smile, one that didn't quite reach her eyes. Despite their obvious attraction to one another, she was wary, he could see that. Of him specifically? Or of all men? "I'd like that."

Dylan settled her son more firmly on his hip as he moved aside to let her walk into the large building. Her eyes widened when she saw the interior of his boathouse. Framed in a classic Craftsman style, the ceiling was three stories high, with large wood-framed windows letting in light on every side. But the best part of the building was, hands down, that the skylights were retractable so that he could work under the open sky.

"Your boathouse is incredible."

He grinned at her awed tone as he pulled a couple of bottles of water out of the fridge in the corner where there was a small kitchen area built in. "Thanks. My brothers and father helped me put it together, although the genius behind the design is my brother Adam."

Before he could give her the water, she caught sight of the nearly completed sailboat in the back of the boathouse and headed toward it as if drawn by a magnet. "How do you do it?" she asked him. "How can you create and build something this amazing?"

"It's all I ever wanted to do. I read everything I could find about making boats as a kid and then once I had the basics down, I started taking them apart. I'd save up my money to buy the junkiest sloops and my parents would let me haul them into their backyard. I'd saw through them, study the hulls, and then I'd try to replicate them as closely as I could."

"Amazing." She reached out to run her hand over the wood before drawing back.

"Go ahead. These things are designed to withstand more than forty knots in an open sea. If it breaks when you put your hands on it," he said with a laugh that drew a giggle out of her little boy, too, "I'm going to have a seriously upset buyer on my hands when the Coast Guard has to come pick him up. Want to touch it, too, Mason?"

Together, the three of them put their hands on the wood, warmed from the sun beaming in from the clear blue sky above.

"I'm Dylan Sullivan, by the way."

Turning away from the boat, she said, "I'm Grace. Grace Adrian."

She held out her hand and when he took it he heard her breath go—easily the sexiest sound he'd ever heard. "It's nice to meet you, Grace. Really nice." But then he frowned slightly. "Your name—it's familiar for some reason. But I'd have remembered if we'd met before."

"We haven't met. I have called you several times, though."

"Right, that's where I know your name from. Sorry about not getting back to you. I'm not great with the phone."

She gave him a look that he could easily read as *No kidding,* before saying, "I hope we didn't interrupt you too badly this morning. I was just really hoping to talk with you for a few minutes. Mason was supposed to stay home today with a babysitter, but she didn't show up, and now we're in the middle of his nap time, which is why he's a little cranky."

"Cranky looks good on him. And now that you're here, what can I help you with?"

She took a deep breath, then pushed her shoulders back as if to ground herself before answering. "I'm a writer and I'd really like to interview you for a story I'm doing on sailing and building boats." Clearly nervous that he'd say no, she continued quickly. "I know you don't do many interviews, but this story isn't going to be about your family, or about money or prestige. Instead, I'm going to write about the heart of a sailor, about loving being on the water, about building boats that help make people's dreams come true. And before you recommend some colleagues that I could talk to instead of you, I need you to know that the editor told me he'll only hire me to write this story if it's about you. And...they need you to be on the cover, too."

"You're right," he said slowly as he let Mason take his ball cap off again to chew on the brim. "I don't normally do interviews. But for you," he said with a smile that he hoped would help settle her worries down, "I'm happy to make an exception. How tight is your deadline?"

She'd looked incredibly relieved when he'd told her he would do the story and cover. But her relief quickly shifted to a slight grimace as she said, "This story is on a pretty tight deadline, I'm afraid. They'll need it and the pictures in four weeks."

"I've got to head out to ferry a boat to a friend in Portland in an hour, but I'll be back Friday afternoon." He also had an upcoming trip to Australia for a major yacht race in a week and a half, but he planned to get to know Grace— and Mason—a heck of a lot better between now and then. "My mom will be making dinner on Friday for the family. Come with me and we can get started then."

She blinked at him in confusion. "You want me to come to your mother's house for our first interview?"

"You and Mason," he clarified. Because even though he wasn't going to make the mistake of freaking her out with his intentions, he also couldn't resist speeding things up a bit by tossing her into the deep end with his family. Dylan just couldn't see waiting...not when he *knew*. "If we get there early, she can watch the baby while you interview me. Unless, of course," he deliberately added to confirm the one thing he needed to be absolutely certain about, "your husband or boyfriend can watch Mason while we talk."

"It's just us."

Knowing it couldn't be easy to raise a baby alone, he tried not to give a whoop of delight that she was single.

"Are you sure your mother will want to watch a little boy she's never met before? Don't you need to ask her first?"

"No," he said with a laugh. "I definitely don't need to ask her if she wants to hang with an awesome kid for a couple of hours. There are few things she loves more. Plus, this way you can ask my family questions for your story." He wasn't usually a steamroller with women—he'd never needed to be when they'd always come to him. But with Grace, he needed to know exactly when he'd see her again. "I'll come pick you guys up at four on Friday?"

Grace stared at him for a few seconds, her expression unreadable, before she finally said, "Okay, that will be fine. And thank you for agreeing to work with me on this story. I really appreciate it."

He didn't need her thanks. Her mouth against his, however, he would gladly take. But since he knew he'd already pushed her enough for one day, he simply said, "I'm looking forward to it, Grace." He liked the sound of her name, the way it felt on his lips. "There's a pad of paper on my desk behind you so that you can give me your address and phone number."

She moved toward the desk against the far wall, and he enjoyed every second of watching her hips sway as she walked in her heels. But halfway to his desk, she stopped and turned to face him. "How many times have you refused to be interviewed for stories like this in the past?"

He shrugged, making Mason giggle when he bounced slightly in Dylan's arms. Bouncing the baby around more on purpose, he said, "Countless. Why do you ask?"

She looked between him and her son, her expression still wary...but also more than a little stunned, too. "I'm just surprised you said yes to me so quickly. Because I really do need to write this cover story about you. So if you're only planning to mess around with me for a laugh—"

"I promise I'm not messing around with you. Not in the slightest." He hoped that one day she'd look back on this conversation and realize that he'd been serious about her and her son even then. "You were right when you said I'd like the angle you're going to take for the story. No one needs to read another story about the fastest way to hoist a spinnaker. But a story about a sailor's heart? That's what it's really all about, whether you're taking a Sunfish out on a Saturday afternoon or you're racing an eight-million-dollar yacht for the World Cup."

"I'm sorry, I didn't mean for my question to come out like that." He could see how tired she was now that she'd let her defenses down just a little bit. "Not when I really am grateful that you're available to do the interview. I just need to be sure that you're really on board with this."

She didn't need to say anything more for him to understand immediately that she'd been screwed over before and had a hard time trusting people when they gave her their word. Probably, it wasn't too much of a stretch to guess, by the guy who had gotten her pregnant.

"I'm not a fan of phones," he told her. "And I don't much care for anything that falls under the category of running a business. But when it comes to giving my word to people? I was raised to stand by it. And I do, Grace. No matter what."

For a few moments she stared at him as if she wasn't sure whether it was safe to believe what he'd just said, before finally turning to head toward his desk again. By the time she returned from writing her address on the pad of paper, she was all business as she reached for Mason.

"We'll get out of your hair now. See you Friday."

It was nearly impossible to keep from dragging her against him for a kiss so that he could see her beautiful skin flush again. But just as he knew not to head a sailboat up into the wind before it was blowing hard enough to point him toward his true destination, he also knew better than to move too fast with Grace.

Not when something told him a far better plan would be to let both of them anticipate that kiss for the next several days, instead.

CHAPTER THREE

Thunder and lightning rocked the sky outside Grace's apartment on Friday afternoon as she waited for Dylan to come pick them up. Mason had crawled over to the window and was clapping with glee every time the lightning flashed and thunder boomed.

Grace lifted him so that he could get a better view of the storm, one that felt way too close to the storm that had been raging inside of her for the past three days. Dylan had deftly maneuvered her into agreeing to do the interview at his childhood home, of all places. While it wasn't at all unusual for a big name to call the shots with a journalist, the fact that she'd taken one look at Dylan and had *wanted* him in a way she'd never wanted another man had her worried.

Very worried, given that the one time she'd let the line blur between her job and her personal life had been a huge mistake.

She hugged Mason tighter as she mentally erased the word *mistake.* She would willingly have made a thousand mistakes all over again to have him here with her. But even though the two of them had made it through both her solo pregnancy and single parenting for the first ten months of his life, that didn't mean she needed to make another, similar mistake with Dylan.

Richard Bentley had asked Grace out during their interview a year and a half ago. No one that charming or full of compliments had ever looked in her direction before. So while she knew she shouldn't mix work with pleasure, he'd been too persuasive and determined for her to resist. Especially in the wake of her father's death only six months earlier. All she'd wanted to do was just forget for a little while.

Her first date with Richard had been on a private rooftop just outside of Washington, D.C. The restaurant with its white tablecloths had been so fancy that she would have felt terribly out of place in her simple black dress and shoes if they hadn't been in a completely private part of the restaurant. By the end of the evening, her head was spinning with bubbly and what had seemed at the time like the most romantic date she'd ever had. She never usually slept with a guy on the first date, but looking back, Grace couldn't deny that she'd felt as though she'd owed Richard for the fairy-tale evening.

On their second date, he'd taken her out on the sailboat, and though the trip hadn't gone as well as dinner under the stars, she hadn't considered ending that date with only a kiss good night, either. Every date they had was the same: He'd take her somewhere private that knocked her socks off and then she'd invite him in for the night. By the time she'd realized that something didn't seem quite right—Why did he never take her out where strangers could see them together? Why did he always have an excuse about being too busy to see her or talk during the week? Why did he say he wanted to keep their relationship between just the two of them for a little while longer?—she'd also missed her period.

Richard hadn't been *at all* pleased to learn just weeks later that she was pregnant.

It should have been crazy for Grace to assume that Dylan had anything more in mind tonight than a quick interview and a home-cooked meal at his parents' house. But she'd stopped being able to lie to herself on the day the pregnancy test had come up positive. So while she couldn't understand it, she also couldn't deny the heat that had been in Dylan's eyes when he'd looked at her. Nor could she deny the answering hit of heat she'd felt simply from being near him. Adding in how good he'd been with Mason and how easily he'd been able to turn her son's tears into giggles? Right there were three big fat reasons why she would need to work overtime to keep things strictly professional. Because he was far, far too tempting...

The doorbell rang, and she tried to prepare herself to see him again, but when she opened the door, the obvious appreciation in his gaze had her long-dormant sensuality immediately leaping back to life, higher and hotter than ever before. Just the way it had on Tuesday in his boathouse.

"You look beautiful, Grace."

"Thank you." It had been so long since anyone had told her she was pretty—or since she'd let herself believe it. "Come on in and I'll go grab Mason's things."

Her son immediately reached for Dylan, and though she felt the same twinge in her chest at the thought of letting anyone else hold him, she knew better than to try to hold Mason off this time. Clearly, he'd been yearning to be close to another guy.

"I like your place," Dylan said as he looked around her apartment's small kitchen and living room. "Having the park across the street must be great."

"It's a great neighborhood, but you're right, the park is what sold me." Despite the fact that the apartment had been, and still was, out of her price range. "Yesterday, when he kept pointing at the slide the big kids were going down, I took him on my lap for the first time."

"I'll bet he loved it, didn't he?"

"So much that we'd still be doing it right now if I hadn't stopped being able to carry him one-armed up the ladder an hour later," she confirmed with a ruffle of Mason's dark hair. She was just about to sling his heavy baby bag and his portable car seat over either shoulder when Dylan said, "Why don't you take a rest from heavy lifting for a couple of hours and let me carry your load for you?"

She didn't know why Dylan's offer made her want to start sobbing, only that she couldn't keep letting him make her go all soft inside like this. Staying tough and determined was what had kept her and Mason's life on track so far. If she let down her guard now, if she let someone else *carry her load* even if it was just for a little while, how hard would it be to pick it up again later, all by herself? Besides, Dylan already had her son in his arms, and she could easily handle the rest. Just the way she always did.

"I've got them," she insisted, when the truth was that between playtime at the park the day before and her long day at the computer rewriting every sentence of her article on new nail polish trends a half-dozen times, her shoulders were aching.

She was more than a little surprised by the beat-up Jeep parked outside her apartment building. From the research she'd done about Dylan's business—and after having been inside his state-of-the-art boathouse—she knew he was wealthy. But unlike her ex, who'd had to proclaim his wealth in any way he could, Dylan obviously didn't feel the need to drive around in a little red sports car or a massive Hummer that would edge out all the other cars on the road.

She quickly fit Mason's car seat into the backseat, then clipped him in and handed him a toy to play with during the drive.

"My mom has been counting down the minutes since I called to let her know that you and Mason were coming to dinner."

Grace had already felt nervous about tonight, but now her nerves jumped another notch. "He was a little fussy earlier. Hopefully he won't melt down right when we get there."

"I'm sure he'll do great tonight. Besides, after raising five of us, my mother's a master at dealing with meltdowns."

With Mason banging away on his toy in the backseat of the Jeep, she should have been able to keep her hormones in check. But the noise didn't make her any less aware of how close to her thigh Dylan's hand was on the gearshift or how good he smelled—an intoxicating combination of the sea and freshly cut wood.

"I'd love to know more about your family." She'd promised Dylan that she wouldn't focus on his family in the story, but just as he'd said on Tuesday, she'd at least need some background on them to help her understand how Dylan had become the man he was. "In doing some preliminary research for my article, I think I have a fairly good handle on what each of them does for a living."

His oldest brother, Ian, was not only the billionaire founder of Sullivan Investments, he had also recently become engaged to Tatiana Landon, a beautiful and talented movie star. Dylan's second-oldest brother, Adam, was well known for his historic house renovations throughout the Pacific Northwest. His middle brother, Rafe, was a private investigator and was engaged to a woman who made gourmet chocolates. Rounding out the group was his sister, Mia, who owned Sullivan Realty and was engaged to rock star Ford Vincent.

"But I was wondering—" At a red light, he turned to smile at her, and her brain mixed up the question she meant to ask and the one she actually wanted to know the answer to. "What's it like to be related to so many famous people?" She clapped her hands over her mouth, shaking her head as though that could magically erase the intrusive words that had fallen out. "I'm sorry, that was out of line. I meant to ask if they all sail, too."

"It wasn't at all out of line," he said with a grin that had only grown wider by the time the light turned green and he hit the gas pedal. "And yes, they all sail, too. Which means that I can usually get them into the water if they ever need to be taken down a notch. There's nothing like the ocean for knocking you around to help you remember that you're only human." He smiled at her again. "But most of the time I forget that they're famous until I'm picking up some milk and see one of their faces on the cover of a magazine. The only time it bothers me is when I see something printed about one of them that isn't true. Which, unfortunately, happens far too often."

"That must be hard."

"None of them are out there for the fame, but they've come to accept that it's part of the dream they're chasing. A rock star like my sister's fiancé, Ford, could never hide out when there are stadiums full of fans around the world who love his music. So they deal with the fame, they handle the spotlight, and when we're together we all forget about it for a little while."

Since she'd already crossed a line, she decided she might as well stay there a little while longer. "Is that why you don't usually do interviews? Because you're afraid the press is going to twist your words around?"

"I'm not a musician or a movie star or a professional baseball player. I'm just a sailor who also makes boats. Anything I've got to say about sailing, someone could figure out for themselves by getting out on the water."

She understood what he was saying, and yet she still couldn't let it go, or keep her mouth shut. "I'm not sure I agree with you. I don't know much about boats beyond what I've read about them for research, but from the pictures I've seen of the ones you've built, and getting to see the one in your boathouse, you're obviously very talented. Just because you're not acting or singing or hitting a baseball doesn't make your gift any less special. Or any less fun to read about for all the people who will never get the chance to sail a boat from one continent to another."

Caught up in making her point, she didn't realize they'd pulled into a driveway in a suburban neighborhood until he turned off the ignition. As a child, her parents had encouraged her to say and do whatever felt right. It was a large part of the reason she'd had the guts to go after writing for a living when it would have been so much safer to get a nine-to-five job in a cubicle. But after allowing herself to be swept away had led to her being pregnant and alone, Grace had decided it would be better to rein in her natural—and wilder—urges.

She gave him a small and slightly rueful smile. "I can get a little carried away sometimes when I feel strongly about something."

"Don't ever apologize for your passion, Grace. Not to me or to anyone. Especially not when you have a way of making a guy look at things differently than he ever has before."

Did he have any idea just how much she'd needed to hear that, especially now that her father wasn't there anymore to remind her to keep taking risks? For the past ten years, her father had been her rock. Her cheerleader. Her main support system. She'd been able to tell him anything and had known that he would keep loving her no matter what, through thick and thin. She'd never imagined that he'd be gone by the time she had her first child. Or that seeing him in the way Mason smiled, in the deep blue of his eyes, would be so bittersweet.

When she looked back up at Dylan, the heat in his gaze made her lips tingle even though he hadn't yet closed the small distance between them and kissed her...which she was almost positive he would have done if Mason hadn't tossed his toy at the dashboard right then, barely missing their heads.

Relief that her son had saved her from herself—along with more regret over missing out on the kiss than she wanted to admit—washed over Grace as she quickly undid her seat belt and picked up the toy.

"If you don't let me at least take the diaper bag this time," Dylan said, "I'll never hear the end of it from my mom."

A few seconds later, she had Mason out of his car seat, Dylan had the heavy bag and the portable high chair, and the three of them were rushing through the rain to his parents' front door. By the time they got to the covered porch, his mother was waiting for them with a big, welcoming smile.

"You must be Grace," his mother said even as Dylan gave her a kiss on the cheek. "I'm Claudia and it's so nice to meet you."

Grace had expected to feel awkward, but Dylan's mother had a way of putting people instantly at ease. "Thank you for having us over tonight, Claudia. This is my son, Mason."

"Hello, Mason," Claudia said, her eyes soft and warm as she looked at the baby. "Aren't you a little cutie? Do you want to come inside and play with some of the toys that have been up in the attic for far too long?"

Right on cue, Mason gave one of his big, one-toothed smiles and reached for her. It was only the second time he'd ever gone to someone else—first to Dylan and now to his mother. What kind of spell did these Sullivans cast over everyone to draw them in so easily and so quickly?

Grace appreciated the way Claudia waited until she'd nodded that it was fine to take Mason into her arms. Maybe tonight wouldn't be quite as nerve-racking as she'd expected. At least until Dylan put his hand on the small of her back as he guided her inside, following his mother into the kitchen.

Just that one small touch scorched through her entire body like a wildfire.

How was she going to make it through a private interview focused on sailing and boat-making, when all she could think about around him was sex?

"Your house is lovely, Claudia."

Grace was surprised, in fact, by how much the Sullivans' house reminded her of the one she'd grown up in. The pretty flowers in vases throughout, the family photos, and even the old dog sleeping on a pillow beneath the piano made it feel cozy. Well loved. Like *home.*

Seeing several pots on the stove and a large array of fruit and vegetables laid out by the cutting board, she said, "I should have realized you'd still be cooking. You don't have to watch Mason." Sure, it would be more difficult to conduct the interview with her son crawling around at their feet wanting to play and be entertained, but she'd find a way to make it work. Plus, she already knew it would be better if she and Dylan weren't alone for too many long stretches, considering it had been hard enough to think straight in the car on the drive over with him sitting so close, even with Mason in the backseat.

But Claudia smiled and said, "I once put on a seven-course dinner while all five kids were running riot through the backyard and the kitchen. I've got this."

And as Grace watched Dylan's mother get down on the floor with Mason to show him how to use the little toy xylophone to make music and he gleefully started banging at the instrument while Dylan's mother laughed delightedly at his antics, she had no doubt whatsoever that Claudia had things covered.

"Can I get you a glass of wine or a beer?" Dylan asked her.

She would *kill* for a glass of wine right now to calm her nerves. But alcohol was the last thing she needed when it was going to take every ounce of self-control she had to keep her walls sturdy and high. "Water would be perfect."

Taking two bottles of water out of the fridge, he said, "There's a covered porch out back where we can talk."

"If you need me for anything, Claudia—"

His mother waved them away. "Go do your interview. Mason and I are going to be just fine, aren't we, cutie?"

His gummy grin was all the answer Grace needed. At least to the question of whether her son would be safe and sound for the next hour or two without her.

As for herself, however—the truth was that as Dylan led her outside toward two seats on the back porch that were set up more with lovers in mind than an interview between strangers, Grace felt anything but safe. Wary, yes. But also undeniably attracted.

And more intrigued by Dylan than she'd been about anyone in a very, very long time.

CHAPTER FOUR

Though it was cool out from the rain still coming down, as Grace got her recorder and notepad out of her bag, her skin was flushed a beautiful rose color that made it nearly impossible for Dylan to keep his hands to himself.

He had spent the past three days ferrying a new boat to a friend in Portland, Oregon, and all the while he'd thought about her. Mason, too. Seventy-two hours of looking at the situation from every angle and he was still in the same place he'd started.

He could easily see himself with both mother and child.

And Grace was still the prettiest woman he'd ever set eyes on.

Dylan had always loved women. The way they smelled. The way they moved. The sweet little sounds they made. But though he'd had as much female companionship as he'd wanted during the fifteen years since he'd hit puberty, he'd never wanted anyone the way he wanted Grace.

And he hadn't even kissed her yet.

His mouth curved up into a grin just thinking about how hot *that* was going to be.

Today Grace would ask him her questions. But soon, he'd want answers from her. Where had she come from? What had her childhood been like? Why was she single instead of married to Mason's father? And who the hell could have been stupid enough to walk away from her and her amazing kid?

If they had been out on his boat right now—the cockpit had always been a damned good confessional and he'd never met anyone who could hold back their true thoughts and feelings at sea—he could have had the answers out of her by the time they got back to the dock. But on land, he'd have to bide his time a little longer. Hopefully not too long, though, given that even the way she tucked her silky hair behind her ear—an ear he very much wanted to nibble on—was incredibly sexy.

She clicked the Record button on the small device on the table between them. "You've told me that sailing is all you ever wanted to do. Sailing and making boats." He loved the sound of her voice, the slightly husky tone that, when combined with her obvious intelligence, made his synapses nearly short out. "I'd love to know why."

He'd expected her to begin with the usual factual or technical questions that journalists had always tried to ask him before: At what age did you start sailing? What was the first boat you made? Why don't you race professionally when you were a superstar at a very young age and could have been at the helm of your own World Cup contender by now?

Instead, she'd just cut straight to the heart of what made him who he was. And he could guess at the reason: This story wasn't just about his heart...it was about hers, too.

"You've sailed before, haven't you?" he asked.

"I've been out on a boat once, but there was hardly time to raise the sails."

"Doesn't matter if it's got paddles or a motor or a jib. Did you like being out on the water?"

She smiled then, dazzling him with her answer before she'd even said it aloud. "I loved it."

"What did you love about it?"

"Everything. The seagulls flying overhead right before we pulled away from the dock, as if they were excited that we were about to join them in their favorite playground. The dark water churning beneath the hull, flexible enough to let us through, yet strong enough to hold us up. The wind against my face, smelling like salt and fish and *life*. The fact that the way the waves rose was utterly unpredictable and yet somehow I felt safer than I ever had before."

"Sometimes," he told her, "when I'm out there hurtling before the wind, and the sky is full of stars, I swear I can hear the mermaids flirting with me."

"I wouldn't be surprised to find out they really were," she said with another smile. One that confirmed that she, too, was tempted to flirt with him. "But what about when it's not so smooth? I know from my research that you've crossed the Atlantic and have sailed thousands of miles in the Pacific, encountering gales and storms, even a couple of hurricanes. How do you keep loving sailing after you've been out there fighting for your boat...and even your life?"

"I like a perfect sail as much as the next person. But the truth is that when the wind whips itself up into a real fury, it can be one of the most beautiful things you'll ever see."

"I can see how a storm could be beautiful, but when you're sailing through one, aren't you scared?"

"Shitless," he confirmed. "In fact, it's usually right when you think you've got it all dialed in, when you're sure that nothing can touch you and the world is your oyster—that's when the wind and the waves decide it's high time to show you just how vulnerable you really are. When you do finally come out on the other side, shaken as all hell, barely able to hold the wheel because every muscle in your body is on the verge of breaking apart, that's when you really know you're alive. And that's also when you remember to appreciate every single moment of it."

"Most people," she said in a soft voice, "would probably think that if there's the potential for that much danger, that much fear, they'd be better off not doing it."

"I don't have kids, obviously, but I imagine it's not that different from the way a parent feels when she lets her baby's hands go so that he can take his first step, or when she leaves him on the first day of kindergarten, or watches him drive away by himself behind the wheel of a car when he's sixteen. Terrified and shaken, but amazed and thrilled at the same time. I wouldn't decide not to have kids and give up all those beautiful moments just because I don't want to have to face some scary ones, too."

Before she could respond, they heard a loud crash followed by Mason's voice rising to meet it. Grace was up out of her seat and running back toward the kitchen so fast that even though Dylan had been on the track team as a teenager, he had barely caught up with her by the time she flew inside the house.

Dylan's mother gave them a slightly guilty look as she pointed to where Mason was sitting in the middle of the kitchen floor surrounded by a half-dozen big pots and pans. He was holding a plastic spatula in each hand and every time he banged them on the pots, he screamed with happiness.

"My kids always loved doing this," his mother said in a voice barely loud enough to carry over the din, "but I forgot how loud it was until a few seconds ago."

Grace still had her hand over her chest as she shook her head. "He's obviously having a fabulous time," she said into the pause between Mason's drumbeats. "I just haven't left him with very many people, so when I heard the loud noise—" She shook her head. "I shouldn't have panicked like that, not when I knew he was in good hands."

But he could see just how much his mother loved Grace's commitment to her son. Just as much as Dylan did himself. He'd always been the most carefree Sullivan. No heavy responsibilities beyond getting a boat from one place to another or putting one together in time to make a customer happy. He'd had girlfriends, of course, but none who had ever had a chance of going beyond the just-having-fun stage. He was there for his family and close friends whenever they needed him for something, of course, but they were a pretty self-sufficient bunch. Dylan had always been able to sail away at a moment's notice, whereas Grace was totally grounded by her responsibility to her son.

"You're a mom," Claudia said. "Panicking is what we're best at."

He was glad when Grace laughed and her expression smoothed out, away from the embarrassment that she'd clearly felt just moments ago.

"I'm happy to keep him entertained if you'd like to go back out and continue with your interview before the others get here. Of course, if you'd like to take him with you—"

"No," Grace interrupted. "He's having a great time with you."

"It's mutual," his mother said with a big smile that spoke to just how much she meant it. "You've absolutely made my day by letting me play with him."

Dylan caught his mother's look as he and Grace headed back outside. One that said, *You're going to make all of my dreams come true with these two, aren't you?*

His silent response was just as clear: *I'm sure as hell going to try.*

CHAPTER FIVE

"Well, aren't you the cutest thing I've ever seen!" a female voice rang out from inside the house a while later. "Who do you belong to?"

Dylan grinned at Grace. "Sounds like my sister and her fiancé are here." He stood and held out a hand for her. "Ready to meet the whole crew?"

Grace took a deep breath before putting her hand into his. "Sure."

When she stood up, he was close. Closer than he'd been before now. For a few heady moments, she couldn't pull her hand away, couldn't stop her heart from beating way too fast.

"I shouldn't leave my things out, just in case the rain blows in."

His eyes moved from hers to her mouth, then back up again. "Good idea."

How was it, she wondered as she tucked her notebook and recorder back inside her bag, that they could be saying nothing and yet so much at the same time? *I shouldn't want you, shouldn't want this,* was what she'd really meant. And she swore he'd answered her in the same way: *It will be good, Grace, if you'll just let it happen. So damned good.*

She was shocked to see that it had been an hour and a half since they'd left Mason banging on the pots and pans in Claudia's kitchen. Yes, she'd loved being out on the water that one time, enough that she'd made a pitch for a story to a sailing magazine, but listening to Dylan talk about sailing, and what it meant to him and other sailors, had quickly filled her with a longing to do more than just write about it.

The same longing had struck her earlier in the week when she'd been looking at the sailboat he was completing in his boathouse. Maybe it was because, from what Dylan had already told her, building a boat wasn't too different from the way she'd taught herself to write. First by taking apart the articles that spoke to her and studying their structure. Then starting to build them on her own, word by word, paragraph by paragraph, page by page.

In any case, the more she learned about what he actually did all day, the more she couldn't blame him for not bothering to pick up his phone. If she were building amazing sailboats, and then sailing them on the open sea, she wouldn't bother, either.

"It's a real skill to ask questions that get straight to the heart of things," Dylan said as they headed for the kitchen. "Where did you learn to do that?"

She was amazed yet again by how easily Dylan gave compliments. Her ex had rarely complimented her on anything but her figure. In fact, now that she thought more about it, she and Richard hadn't had many conversations about anything that really mattered. The truth was that they'd never had a true connection.

"My parents said that even when I was a little girl, I had a million questions about everything. Journalism was always a perfect fit for me, just like sailing is for you. But I have to say that for a guy who doesn't like doing interviews, you made it really easy for me today."

He held the door open for her and she saw a stunning woman down on the floor stacking blocks alongside Mason.

"Hi, I'm Mia. And your son is the cutest thing I've ever seen."

"I agree," Grace said with a smile. "I'm Grace, and it's nice to meet you. Thanks for keeping him so entertained."

She looked up just then to see Ford Vincent walking toward her with his hand outstretched. Despite knowing the rock star might be here tonight with Mia, given that she was his fiancée, Grace still came *this close* to freezing up with shock.

"Hi." Somehow she managed to get her hand into his without shaking or sweating or doing any number of other embarrassing things. Not, however, that she was rewarded for that with a reprieve, because literally a moment later, Tatiana Landon came into the room.

"Tatiana," Dylan said, "this is Grace and her son, Mason."

The movie star looked pleasantly surprised—*delighted* would be a better word for it, actually—by their presence. "It's lovely to meet you. I can't wait to hear all about how you and Dylan met. He never brings anyone to dinner."

Oh no, they all assumed she was dating him. "Actually, we're just—"

Before she could finish her sentence, Mason tossed a block across the room, nailing a man in a suit right in the knee.

She dashed over to pick it up, but the blindingly good-looking man beat her to it. He was smiling as he handed the block to her. "Your son has a great arm."

"No kidding," Dylan agreed, the grin in his voice clear without her needing to see it. "You should have seen Mason toss his toy in front of my boathouse earlier this week."

The man raised his eyebrows at this tidbit before turning back to Grace and saying, "I'm Dylan's brother Ian."

She had never been comfortable as the center of attention and could feel her composure, which had been shaky at best a few minutes ago, rapidly shredding to pieces as they all stared at her, especially this brother whose gaze was just a bit more intense than that of the others.

"I'm so glad you and your son were able to come to dinner with all of us tonight." Right on cue, Mason chucked another block at Ian, upon which he bent down to gently lob it back at Mason's feet.

When Mason giggled with glee at having another new friend to play with, Claudia said, "Isn't Mason great? I had the privilege of watching him for the past couple of hours while Grace and Dylan did their interview."

Another couple walked into the kitchen. "Dylan actually agreed to do an interview?" asked the dark-haired man who looked so much like Dylan. "Has the apocalypse come?"

"Meet Rafe and Brooke," Dylan said as Mason crawled over to his feet and lifted his arms. Without pause, Dylan picked him up. "I'd like you guys to meet Grace and Mason."

When Brooke waved at the baby, he gleefully waved right back. "Isn't he sweet?" Mia said as Ford helped her up to stand in what looked to Grace like impossibly high heels.

"So sweet," Brooke and Tatiana both agreed.

The way everyone immediately fell in love with her son helped Grace regain a little of her composure. Of course, that was right when one more brother walked in, saw Mason with his sleepy little head resting on Dylan's shoulder, and asked, "Whoa, did you adopt a kid on your last sailing expedition?"

"Grace, this is Adam. I'm sure you're going to be really surprised to hear that he's still single."

That was when Adam turned and saw her. "The baby's yours?" When she nodded, he gave her a really flirtatious grin. "No wonder the kid is so cute."

By then, what else could she do but laugh? Dylan had talked during their interview about learning to walk on the deck of a sailboat during a storm without being tossed off. Now she thought she knew exactly what that felt like simply from having met his entire family in the past five minutes.

Or nearly the entire Sullivan clan, because when a handsome man with gray hair came in and every person in the room beamed at him, she now knew exactly how handsome Dylan would be in thirty years—and also how much the children he'd have would adore him. And when Dylan's father took Claudia into his arms and kissed her, Grace couldn't hold back her sigh at how sweet it was to see two people so much in love after so many years.

No wonder there was so much love in the house.

Normally, Mason would be tired and cranky by now, but he was completely in his element with all the women cooing over him and all the men saying he was probably going to be a pro ball player with an arm like his.

Of the two of them, she was the one overwhelmed, not only with her feelings for the subject of her magazine story, but also by his magnificent family. So when Claudia asked if Grace could help her put together the salad, she was thrilled to be able to step out of the big group. Their mother, Grace had already figured out, was the calm eye at the center of the storm.

"Thank you, again, for watching Mason while I interviewed Dylan."

"Anytime you need someone to watch your son, you know who to call. He's all changed and clean, by the way. Did your interview go well?"

"Listening to Dylan talk, I felt almost as if I were out there in a sailboat with him. Your son is a fascinating man."

Grace looked up from the cucumber she was slicing to sneak a glance at him. Only to find that he was already looking at her. Flustered again, she had to steady her hands before she resumed work with the knife.

"Mason reminds me of the way Dylan was as a child," Claudia told her. "Sweet. Always ready to laugh." He was laughing right then in Brooke's arms as she bounced him. "Happy to spend hours building things. In fact, he was so easygoing that we realized it would be really easy to leave him be, especially when his brothers and Mia all seemed to need us more. So when Max saw that he was fascinated by sailboats, we both decided we would learn how to sail with him. It was, truly, one of the best things we've ever done, because that's when we really got to know our son...and he got to know us, too."

"In the cockpit confessional," Grace said with a smile, referencing one of the things Dylan had said to her during their interview. "So do you also believe that you can't keep a secret when you're out on a boat?"

"You'll find out for yourself the first time you go sailing with him."

Just then, Mason let out a little wail, and she hurried over to take him from Brooke. "I think he misses his mommy," Brooke said.

Grace pressed a kiss to his forehead. "It's been a big day for him, meeting so many new people." For both of them. "He's probably hungry and thirsty, too." She reached into his bag nearby for a bottle. He cuddled into her chest and started drinking like he'd just crossed the Sahara Desert.

Dylan brought them over to the dining table, where he pulled out a chair next to his. She'd intended to put Mason in his portable high chair, but after he had his bottle he crawled into Dylan's arms and immediately dozed off.

It was, Grace thought, the cutest, sweetest thing she'd *ever* seen—a big, strong man holding a sleeping baby so gently. One who obviously felt so safe that Mason wasn't the least bit disturbed by everyone else coming into the dining room, laughing and teasing each other in the way only a truly close family could. Grace noted that she wasn't the only one who thought Dylan and Mason painted a beautiful picture— she was pretty sure Claudia's eyes got a little glossy, too.

Heaping platters of food were passed around, and with Dylan's hands full, Grace filled both their plates with some of everything. She thought she'd be too nervous to eat in a group of famous strangers, but the minute she took her first bite of his mother's delicious food, she realized she was starving.

Sitting down with everyone at dinner finally gave Grace a chance to study his family a bit. Still a little star struck, at the same time she was amazed by how *normal* they seemed. They joked, they teased, they flirted—especially Adam. From what Dylan had told her, they all got together on a regular basis.

Tatiana, who was sitting on her left, said, "I'd love to know more about the story you're writing, Grace. Especially since Dylan is usually so reluctant to be interviewed."

More than a little surprised that Tatiana didn't seem the least bit wary around her because she was a journalist, Grace told her, "It's a piece about the heart of a sailor and why people are drawn to getting out on an ocean that can be both beautiful and dangerous. I've read a ton about sailing this week, but two hours with

Dylan has been more helpful than an entire library of books would have been."

"It sounds fascinating," Tatiana said. "I've always admired people who are skilled at culling a ton of information into just the parts that matter. What's your secret?"

"Brilliant questions," Dylan answered.

"Endless questions, anyway," Grace said. "If you hadn't all shown up for dinner, I would probably still be peppering Dylan with them."

"So you're not done with him yet?" Mia asked.

Mason shifted in Dylan's arms so that he was halfway in hers, too, and Grace focused on helping him get more comfortable as she replied, "Not even close. The two of us have still got a lot of ground to cover."

When she looked up, everyone was grinning like crazy. What had she just said to make all of them look so happy?

Fortunately, that was when the conversation changed to their cousin Ryan's winning pitch at last night's baseball game, so Grace finally let herself relax into her seat. As much as she could relax, anyway, with Dylan's thigh pressed against hers beneath the crowded dining table.

With her son sleeping on both of their laps and his family right there, too, she shouldn't have had to keep fighting back her desire for him.

But she did.

CHAPTER SIX

"Since everyone is here tonight," Mia said when everyone had finally eaten their fill, "Ford and I want to talk with you about something we've been thinking a lot about."

"Please tell me it doesn't have anything to do with weddings," Adam begged, looking trapped. "I swear that's all any of you talk about anymore."

"Actually," she said with a wide smile, "our wedding is *exactly* what we want to talk about with all of you." Ian and Mia shot each other a look that read to Grace like a secret, silent code between brother and sister.

Meanwhile, Adam informed Dylan, "It's just the two of us left now." A moment later, however, when his gaze flashed to Grace and Mason, he shook his head, then picked up his beer and took a long pull.

"As most of you know," Mia continued, "I've been planning my wedding since I was a little girl." When Adam groaned again, his sister socked him in the shoulder. "I always thought the bigger the better, probably at an exotic destination with a week-long party on an island. But now..." Mia paused when Ford threaded his fingers through hers and lifted them to his lips while they shared a look so loving Grace could feel it in the center of *her* chest.

"Now all we want," Ford finished for her, his voice just as deep and mesmerizing as it was when he was singing one of his hit songs, "is to have our family with us. We had thought about getting married up at the lake, but we don't want to take away from Rafe and Brooke's special day this summer."

"Of course you should get married at the lake," Brooke immediately protested, but instead of agreeing with her, Rafe pressed a kiss to his fiancée's forehead. "Something tells me they've already got something else in mind."

Ian cleared his throat. "Sounds to me like the two of you are ready to say your vows, aren't you?"

Dylan's oldest brother looked and sounded truly choked up, not at all as if he were teasing. And when Mia's eyes also filled as she nodded, Grace barely held in her gasp of surprise.

Oh my God, Mia and Ford weren't about to get married tonight, were they?

"That's exactly what we're ready for," Mia confirmed. "Ford and I don't want to wait any longer. And we don't want to have a big circus of a wedding with helicopters and paparazzi. We'll have a big party later for everyone to come to, but for tonight, we just want you guys."

Tears were already streaming down Claudia's face by the time she made it around the table to throw her arms around her daughter and her soon-to-be son. "I can't believe you all planned this in secret! A wedding right here in our living room." Dylan's mother sounded overwhelmed. And absolutely thrilled.

Grace was so stunned by what was about to happen that it wasn't until Dylan started to help her out of her seat that she realized she was still sitting at the dining room table gaping over the fact that one of the biggest rock stars in the world was about to have a totally secret wedding in front of her!

But despite how shockingly cool all this was—how amazing did a family have to be to actually do something like this?—the unavoidable truth was that she was intruding on a private family moment.

She turned to Dylan. "Mason and I shouldn't—"

"Stay." He reached for her hand, his expression so full of warmth that her heart, already swelling with the heady romance swirling throughout the room, skipped a beat. "Please."

By the time she finally managed to look away from his mesmerizing eyes, Ian was standing with his back to the big stone fireplace.

Mia and Ford were holding hands in front of him, while the rest of the family gathered around them...and Grace knew there was nowhere else she'd rather be.

* * *

Dylan knew none of them would ever forget this wedding. Not only because Mia, Ford, and Ian had sprung it on them all so brilliantly, but because of a baby who suddenly decided he was done napping and wasn't the least bit happy about how quiet everyone else was being.

As Grace took Mason from him and tried to rock him back to sleep, Adam and Rafe were trying not to laugh. Dylan would have been right there with them both were it not for the fact that he could see Grace panicking as she tried to soothe her little boy, to no avail.

He reached out for Mason's little hand and stroked it softly to try to get his attention. As plump wobbly lips and eyes that were just starting to fill with tears met his, Dylan widened his eyes and stuck out his tongue. Thankfully, soon Mason was imitating him by sticking out his little tongue and giggling.

"I'll take him outside," Grace whispered as she started to move away from the rest of the group, but Mia was already saying, "This is so perfect, saying our vows while the cutest baby ever giggles at the silly faces everyone is making at him." She looked back at Ford. "I want one of those. Soon."

He leaned over to kiss her, but even though he spoke in a low voice, they could all hear him say, "We'll get started tonight."

Adam groaned again as the two lovebirds clearly forgot there was anyone else in the living room with them. "Ian, I think that's your cue to get started."

With a grin and a nod, Ian began. "We're here tonight to witness the joining of a man and woman who have proved beyond a shadow of a doubt not only that they are meant to be together, but also that they have what it takes to make love last. All any of us have ever wanted for you, Mia, is happiness and true love. Knowing that you've found that with Ford makes this one of the best moments of our lives, and we're thrilled to be able to share in your vows with each other tonight."

Dylan could hear Grace's breath hitch in her throat as emotion swamped her, and he reached out to put his hand over hers.

Ford brought both of Mia's hands up to his mouth and pressed a kiss to them before he began to speak. "You are everything to me, Mia. My dreams. My heart. My soul. Every day when I wake up with you beside me, then fall asleep with you in my arms, I know I'm the luckiest man alive." He pressed a kiss to each of her cheeks, wet with tears, before kissing her on the mouth. "I can't wait to have forever with you."

Mia had never looked happier than she did right then as she smiled at Ford, even while her tears continued to fall.

"I always knew I wanted what my parents had." Mia turned to smile at their mom and dad, who were holding tightly to each other, their hearts in their eyes as they watched their youngest say her vows. "A love so deep and true that nothing could ever come between them. I was so sure I knew what that love would look like when it came. I had it all planned out—the perfect guy who would say all the right things and sweep me away like a princess in a perfect fairy tale. But then, there you were. Not out of a fairy tale, but better. Because you are real. Raw. Honest. And with a heart so big that I'm constantly astounded by everything you are and everything you do. Especially the way you love me without holding anything back. I can't wait to be your wife, Ford."

When they turned back to Ian, he was clearly working to pull himself together so that they could finish the ceremony. "Mia, do you freely and without reservation give yourself to Ford in marriage?"

"I do." Mia slid Ford's wedding band on his left hand. "With this ring, I am yours and you are mine. Wear this ring forever as a sign of our love."

"Ford, do you freely and without reservation give yourself to Mia in marriage?"

"I do." Ford reached into his pocket for a simple platinum wedding band and put it on Mia's ring finger. "I give you this ring to wear with love and joy. As this ring has no end, our love is also forever."

"May the wedding rings you exchanged today remind you always that you are surrounded by enduring love. And now, by the power vested in me by the City of Seattle, it is my honor and delight to declare you husband and wife. You may seal this declaration with a kiss."

And as the new husband and wife kissed to seal the deal, Mason let out a whoop that had all of them joining in.

CHAPTER SEVEN

A couple of hours later, they carried Mason and all his things up the stairs to her apartment. Earlier, she'd planned to say a simple thank you and good night to Dylan at the end of the evening. But after the evening they'd just shared, one full of love and family and promises of forever, nothing seemed clear cut to Grace anymore.

Nothing except the fact that she wasn't ready for the night to be over.

"If you don't mind waiting for me to tuck Mason in, I'd be happy to make us some coffee."

"Sounds good." He ran his hand lightly over her son's head. "Good night, buddy."

She took Mason into the bedroom the two of them shared, put him into a dry diaper, and zipped him into soft blue jammies. When she whispered, "Sweet dreams, baby," he finally woke enough to turn his mouth to hers for a smooch. Her heart overflowed with love as she kissed him, then tucked him into his crib, his favorite stuffed giraffe in his hand, his blanket over the little butt he immediately stuck up into the air when he rolled onto his stomach.

Knowing she couldn't go back out to Dylan feeling this soft, this vulnerable, she went into her en suite bathroom to brush her hair and splash some cold water on her face. Unfortunately, the woman who stared back at her didn't look at all like a professional journalist. On the contrary, with eyes that bright and skin that flushed, she looked far more like a woman who was falling head over heels for the gorgeous man in her living room.

She gave herself a mental and physical shake. She couldn't do that. *Wouldn't* do that. Not when there was a little boy sleeping just a few feet away who depended on her to protect him. She was done making mistakes with good-looking, wealthy men.

Grace had always trusted her instincts, at least until she'd fallen for Richard. After having gotten things so horribly wrong with him, she'd been keeping her guard up, to protect both herself and her son.

She'd never be able to forget what his parents had said to her when they'd paid her a surprise visit the day after she'd told Richard about her pregnancy: *"Our son has a weakness for inappropriate girls like you, unfortunately. But his temporary mistake cannot become a permanent stain on our family."* She'd been stunned when the esteemed former senator and his wife had handed her two certified checks drawn on an account with no identifiers on it. One for an abortion...and the other as payment for her silence. She'd started planning her move that same day, to a city as far away from Washington, D.C., as she could get.

But as wealthy and powerful as the Bentleys were, Grace was pretty sure that the Sullivans were even more so. Would any of them ever deal with "accidents" in this way? By buying off and burying them?

She couldn't imagine that they would, couldn't wrap her head around any of the men or women she'd met tonight doing anything that terrible. Then again, how could she know for sure? After all, she'd only just met them all. And hadn't Richard snowed her, too?

As renewed wariness crept back into her, she decided it was good that Dylan was still here. That way, she could make it perfectly clear before he left that the two of them were never going to move beyond the story she was writing.

Because even if Dylan and his family were as good, as honest and kind, as they'd seemed tonight, the truth was that it would only make things harder. Maybe if Dylan had been like his architect brother and Realtor sister, whose lives were about putting down permanent roots, then that fantasy might have had a chance of coming true. But if she'd learned anything during her two-hour interview this afternoon on his parents' back porch, it had been that the man on the other side of her bedroom door was meant to sail away wherever the wind took him, whenever it started blowing. Once upon a time, she might have been able to believe in fantasy happy-ever-afters and go with him. But she couldn't do that now. Building a safe, loving home for Mason was her top priority.

Looking up into the mirror, she saw that the brightness on her face was now gone. In its place was acceptance...and determination not to get swept up in attraction or romance.

"Sorry that took me so long," she said when she returned to the living room. "I needed to get Mason changed before tucking him in." Not to mention the time it had taken to get her head back on straight.

"It gave me time to admire your pictures."

Dylan was standing in front of one from the day Mason had been born. Seven pounds, two ounces, wrapped in the hospital's swaddling blankets, he'd been red-faced and hairless. Grace still remembered how awed she'd been by the life she'd created...and how terrified she was at the thought of taking him home all by herself.

"It was the best day of my life."

"I'll bet it was." She could feel Dylan's eyes on her now, instead of the picture. "Everyone in my family loved the two of you. Just the way I knew they would."

"Your family is fabulous," she said as she walked into her small adjoining kitchen to put the coffee on. "Mason was in heaven playing with everyone. And they were all so kind, even when he almost ruined your sister's wedding."

"He didn't come anywhere close to ruining anything. Trust me, Mia meant it when she said it was her perfect wedding."

Grace knew she needed to get serious with Dylan, but there was something she needed to tell him first. "Tonight was amazing. Mia and Ford's wedding was the most beautiful one I've ever been to. They're so perfect for each other, and the fact that your brother Ian officiated made it even better."

"Mia's always had a knack for doing things her own way." She could hear how much he loved his sister in his voice, see the obvious affection in his eyes. "I'd say the wedding tonight was exactly right for her and Ford."

"It was *beautiful.* Did you really not know anything about it?"

"Nope, nothing. Ian and Mia have always been especially close, so it's not surprising that they'd have cooked this up. They would have known how much my parents would love it, too, more than having to contend with hundreds of strangers and paparazzi everywhere."

Grace had never really understood the pressure that someone like Ford might have to deal with until tonight. Obviously, none of the Sullivans was complaining about their good fortune, but it definitely added another layer to why Dylan might choose to keep his distance from the press. She sincerely hoped her story about him didn't end up opening a can of worms for him.

"Your parents really did love it," Grace said with a smile as she handed Dylan a cup. "Everyone was so happy that even Mason couldn't resist cheering at the end." And she hadn't been able to resist moving into Dylan's arms to hug him and share in the joy all around her.

Remembering how warm, how good, it had felt to be in his arms, jolted her into realizing that all this wedding talk had veered her even further toward the personal. Knowing she needed to build up her professional boundaries once more, she made herself circle back to the real reason she and Dylan were spending time together.

"I hope I didn't worry you when I told your family that an article like this often takes more than one in-depth interview for me to put it together. I won't take up too much of your time, though."

"Whatever you need, just let me know," he said with one of his easy grins, the epitome of the carefree sailor. "Are you free tomorrow?"

Surprised that he was that excited about moving forward with their story, she said, "I need to transcribe the recording of our interview before I can ask you any intelligent questions during round two. Monday would probably be better."

"Monday's fine for the interview, but tomorrow night I'd like to take you and Mason to an aquarium for kids that one of my friends owns. From what I know of your little guy, and how curious he is about everything, I'm pretty sure he'd get a huge kick out of sticking his hands into the tanks to touch the sea creatures."

"We can't." The two words were some of the hardest she'd ever said, when she knew that not only would Mason *love* to play at that aquarium, but also that going with Dylan would make it even better for him.

"How about Sunday, then?"

"No, that isn't what I mean." Her apartment was way too small for the sparks that were jumping between the two of them, despite her most determined efforts to douse them. "We both had a great time with you tonight, but from now on I think we should only see each other when we're working on the story."

"You told me you don't have a husband, and that there's no boyfriend, either."

"There isn't."

"You, me, Mason—we all get along pretty well, don't you think?"

"Yes, but that isn't the point."

"Then tell me what is, Grace. Tell me why you won't let me take you and Mason out to have some fun tomorrow night after both of us have finished our work for the day."

In less than sixty seconds, Dylan had transformed from carefree to utterly determined. She should have seen it coming, should have realized that anyone who could pilot a forty-foot sailboat through dangerous and unpredictable seas would have more determination in his little finger than most people could even comprehend.

And in that moment, she realized that was precisely what Dylan was. *Dangerous.* Because for as sweet as he was with Mason, with her, with his family...he was also incredibly, shockingly dangerous to her peace of mind. To her future.

She thought she'd wanted him on Tuesday when she'd first met him at his boathouse, and then again tonight when he'd picked them up. But that was nothing compared to how much she wanted—*needed*—him now. Despite a past that had taught her to know better.

She was so flustered, the first thing that came out of her mouth was, "If we spend too much time together, I might not be able to remain objective about my story."

"I'm not sure I see how objective you have to be about some guy who likes sailing and boats." His gaze went too deep, saw too much. But she still couldn't look away. "That's not why you think you need to keep your distance, is it?"

All afternoon, she'd asked him to tell her the truth about his life, about his love for sailing. And after witnessing his honest love for his family firsthand, how could she possibly lie to him now? "No, that's not the real reason."

"One day," he said in a gentle voice, after the silence had drawn out between them for several long moments, "I hope you'll trust me enough to tell me what it is."

She hadn't talked to anyone about what had happened, hadn't wanted her old friends to know what an idiot she'd been by falling for promises her ex hadn't actually ever made. Nor had she wanted anyone to know who the father of her child was, just in case the Bentleys decided they wanted Mason after all. It had been easier just to disappear the day after they'd given her the checks. To take a trip across the country, seeing all the sights she and her parents had always talked about visiting one day, before finally settling in Seattle when the water had called to her.

And yet, even though she shouldn't feel as if she knew Dylan well enough, everything she'd been through over the past year and a half suddenly wanted to come spilling out.

"Does Mason usually sack out at eight o'clock?" When she nodded, he said, "Then how about I pick you up at five so we'll have a good couple of hours at the aquarium before he gets too sleepy to enjoy himself?"

"Didn't you hear what I just said? I can't date you."

"It won't be a date. Just three new friends hanging out."

She knew she should say no, but now that she'd been perfectly clear with Dylan that they weren't going to start anything romantic, was there really any harm in spending a couple of hours together at an aquarium? Especially when she knew how much fun Mason would have with the sea creatures and Dylan.

Of course, even as she rationalized, the wanting was humming away inside of her, calling her a liar. *Just admit you want to be with him, that you want his mouth, his hands, on you. That you've been wondering all night what it would be like to kiss him.*

"Doesn't the aquarium close at five?"

His grin told her how pleased he was that he was on the verge of getting what he wanted, even if she hadn't quite said yes yet. "I'll trade my buddy a sail to keep it open a couple of hours longer for us."

With that, he took both of their cups over to the sink and rinsed them out, a man who had clearly been raised not to expect anyone to wait on him. She stood, too, hoping it wasn't going to be awkward when they said good night.

"Thanks for a really great interview and for introducing me to your family. I really did have a good time tonight."

"I did, too, friend," he said as he headed out her door. "See you tomorrow night."

Another man might have pressured her into being more, but Dylan had made her laugh instead with his use of *friend*.

"You were a handful as a kid," she said, "weren't you?"

At the bottom of the steps, he laughed, too. "Why do you think my parents were always so happy to see me sailing away?"

Closing the door behind her, Grace knew she had no right to feel disappointed that he'd left without even trying to sneak a kiss. He was simply doing what she'd asked him to do: treating her like a friend instead of a potential girlfriend. But she had barely slid the bolt closed when she heard footsteps and then a knock.

"You're back." She looked up into his eyes, an even deeper, darker brown than usual, as all the butterflies came right back.

He held out her bag with her notebook and recorder. "You forgot this in my car."

"Oh." Her voice was flat, heavy with disappointment she couldn't figure out how to hold back. "Thanks. I would have been in trouble without this tomorrow."

"It doesn't feel right to me, either," he said softly.

Doesn't feel right? "You don't want to work with me on this story?"

"No, the story is fine. Leaving like this, like you don't mean anything more to me than just some journalist, that's what feels wrong." He reached for her hand with his free one, just that one simple touch sending heat searing through her. "I was trying so hard tonight to play it cool, to not scare you away by coming on too strong. But all I've ended up feeling like is a liar. And I can't stomach the thought of lying to you,

Grace." He stroked a thumb across her palm, making her shiver despite the heat swamping her system. "So here's the truth—I've wanted to kiss you from the first moment I set eyes on you, and every moment we're together, I only want it more. But, damn it, I won't do anything to hurt you when I know someone else already has. So if you don't want to me to kiss you, and if I've somehow read everything wrong since Tuesday when I could have sworn we already had a connection, tell me now...and I'll make myself go without learning if your mouth tastes as good as it looks."

His touch, his good looks, even her intense attraction to him hadn't been enough to send her over the edge. But when he told her he wouldn't steal a kiss that might hurt her—that was when her defenses fell all the way. Especially when she was still flying from the beautiful wedding at his parents' house.

He was making this *her* choice. Not one that came from guilt. Or because she felt like she owed him a kiss after the evening they'd just shared. But simply because she wanted to know his taste, too.

One kiss with Dylan didn't have to mean forever. It didn't even have to be a promise of more. And maybe if they kissed now, it would keep them from blowing it out of proportion during the rest of their interview.

So instead of grabbing her bag, she grabbed him.

Sliding her hands into his dark hair, she pulled his mouth down to hers and poured all of her pent-up hunger, and need, and wonder at the beauty of the wedding she'd been a part of tonight into the kiss. For a few precious moments, she let herself give in to the madness, to the fiercest, sweetest desire she'd ever known as she nipped at his lower lip with her teeth, then met his tongue with the wet slick of her own. He moved close enough that she could feel the heat and the strength of him all along the front of her body. She drank in his groan, breathed in his clean masculine scent, gloried in his hard muscles pressed against the length of her.

Her head spun with the taste of him, her blood heated with desire, and her chest clenched with desperate need. She wanted more—so much more that she was flat-out stunned by her need for him—and, just for a few moments more, couldn't stop herself from taking their kiss even deeper as a low hum of pleasure sounded in her throat.

Both of them were breathing hard by the time she managed to get a tenuous grip on herself and draw back. She'd never seen eyes so dark, so filled with desire. Eyes that watched her so carefully, as if he was afraid she'd spook. But after all she'd been through over the past couple of years, she decided she would let herself have this one perfect kiss. And she wouldn't regret it.

Even if they could never have a second.

Desperate not to make a big deal out of it, she tried to joke, "If you sail as well as you kiss, no wonder you're a boating legend."

His hands were still on her hips as he said, "You'll find out soon."

"You want to take me sailing?" The thought thrilled and worried her in equal measure. She knew he was right, that she should experience for herself being on one of his boats with him. Unfortunately, something told her that it was going to be really, really difficult to keep her secrets—and Mason's—their own while out on the ocean with Dylan.

"You can't write this story without sailing with me at least once."

"Once I understand more about what you do and about your boats, I'll join you for a sail. But it would probably be best if it took place as our final interview." That way she'd have plenty of time to brace herself against the power of the cockpit confessional.

"Would that really be best?" he asked. "To wait that long?"

She knew he wasn't just talking about sailing anymore, even as she said, "I really think it would." The easiest thing would have been to lean in for another kiss. Easy and oh so good. But she'd stopped being able to take the easy road a year and a half ago. "Good night, Dylan."

His hands tightened on her hips for a split second, sending shivers through her entire body before he finally let her go. "Good night."

And the craziest thing of all was that, despite knowing she needed to keep a tight rein on her heart, Grace couldn't remember ever having had a better one.

CHAPTER EIGHT

Few things, few places, were better than a sunny Saturday morning at the harbor. Families gathered to take out the boats that had been docked all week, dogs barked and played, people's laughter skipped along the glassy surface of the water.

Dylan was back from a quick sail around the Sound by nine and had been working since then on the twenty-four-foot sloop. All the boats he'd built had been a labor of love, but none more than this one. He'd told his family the boat was for a buyer out of San Francisco. But it was actually a surprise for his brothers, his sister, their mates and their kids. He was more than happy to have them use his boats any time they wanted to, but he wanted them to have a sailboat of their own. One where he'd personally laid every plank, pounded every nail. He'd turned down several lucrative boatbuilding contracts in the past couple of months and would happily have turned down more if he hadn't been at the tail end of the build now.

He had rock 'n' roll blasting—courtesy of his new brother-in-law, Ford Vincent—while the sun streamed in through the boathouse doors and the open skylights overhead. Today was especially sweaty work. Sweaty and satisfying. Just like sex, he thought with a grin as he wiped his face dry with the T-shirt he'd taken off a while ago.

Man, that kiss last night...

Dylan had to stop and take a few seconds to relive the moment when Grace's lips had touched his. Everything had gone so hot so fast that he'd had to scramble to catch up. He'd wanted to possess, to brand, to never let go of her soft curves. If he could have lingered over their first kiss, he would have. Instead, as her body strained against his, with only his mouth on hers, he'd ravaged her.

And she'd done exactly the same thing to him.

For as hot as he'd been from the heat of the day and sun pouring in over him, thinking about Grace now had Dylan burning up enough that he needed to grab a Coke and stand on the dock for a few minutes to let the breeze cool him down.

He took in the sun glinting off the water and the boats, the sound of the seals barking playfully at each other, the smell of sunscreen and sea air as a mother and daughter headed out into the bay on a Laser. It was a small boat compared to the yachts owned by the rich and famous of the Pacific Northwest, but it was a classic. A Laser was the first boat his dad had sailed with him. Max Sullivan loved the water, but he wasn't a natural sailor, even if he understood the technicalities of sailing to the finest detail. It was a windier day than a couple of beginners should have been out in, but Dylan had learned fast and had kept them from turtling.

It had been a thrill handling the rigging, learning to tack, holding the tiller, flying across the water. Even better when it started to turn, when he'd had to save them from going over. He'd always enjoyed an easy sail, one where he could just stretch out in the sun and let his mind wander, but right from that first sail he'd known that it was easy to sail well in perfect conditions; it was when the ride started getting rocky that the stronger wills rose to victory.

Even after the kiss he and Grace had shared, Dylan knew she was sure nothing could work between them. Tonight's trip to the aquarium would be another step in proving to Grace that she could trust him not only to be her and her son's friend, but hopefully so much more, too.

He was determined to prove this to her, one perfect kiss at a time...

He might have felt a little bad about throwing her into the deep end last night with his family were it not for the facts that (a) they were awesome, and (b) if all went well with them she would be getting to know his brothers and sisters and parents anyway, so why not do it sooner rather than later? And it had been really good to see how well she fit in with them all despite her initial nerves. In fact, while she'd been helping his mother in the kitchen for a few minutes, Rafe had pulled him aside.

"I never thought that when you finally fell for a woman, it would be one with a kid you'd have to be home for," his brother had said. "But there's something about Grace—and her baby is pretty cute, too. You thinking about hanging up the sails for a while?"

"Families sail around the world all the time," had been Dylan's reply. "Until then, it'll be great to be home more."

Rafe's eyebrows had gone up, then. "You're really serious about her, aren't you?" When Dylan had nodded, Rafe had asked, "How long has this been brewing?"

Dylan had grinned and said, "We met on Tuesday," then went to help Grace and Mason get seated at the dining table while his brother's head spun. It was always fun to throw his siblings off, especially over something they'd never seen coming.

He was just heading back inside when his phone rang. The sight of his parents' number on the caller ID screen made him break his usual rule to ignore it when he was working.

"Dylan, sweetie," his mother said, a smile in her voice, "I'm so glad you picked up."

"For you, always. That was some Friday night dinner, wasn't it?"

His mother gave a happy sigh. "It was just wonderful. Beyond wonderful." He could tell that she was tearing up even now. "Can you believe how sneaky your brother and sister are, cooking up a surprise wedding between them?"

"Sure can. In fact, one time they—" Dylan reconsidered spilling the beans at the last second. "Actually, never mind. It was twenty years ago, but you're probably still better off not knowing. I wouldn't want you to have to ground the newlywed. Especially after she and Ian just pulled off the wedding coup of the century."

When Dylan had called Mia and Ford earlier to congratulate them again, they had been on their way to the airport for an impromptu Hawaiian honeymoon. They'd brought the champagne and roses that he'd sent over for their private plane. Still, for as much as she'd loved the wedding, he knew that wasn't why his mom was calling.

"I absolutely adored Grace and Mason."

"I knew you would. Especially when you saw how cute her son was."

"You five were the cutest babies I'd ever seen, but I have to tell you, Mason slipped right up there into the running last night. He's so sweet and curious and loves meeting and playing with people. And I also noticed that he was particularly partial to you, with the way he kept climbing up into your arms."

"We bonded earlier this week when they came by my boathouse. The three of us are heading out tonight to the hands-on aquarium."

"On a date?" He could hear the hope in her voice.

"Last night was an interview. Tonight we're going to be friends. I'm trying not to move too fast." It was one of the hardest things he'd ever done, holding himself back when he wanted Grace so badly...and knew, even before their smoking-hot kiss, that she wanted him just as badly.

"She's careful," his mother mused. "Or trying to be, at least. She's obviously been hurt."

Knowing he would never forgive himself if he hurt her in any way, he said, "I'll be careful with her, Mom."

"I know you will. Although, honestly, I'm not sure that careful is always the right way to go. Take your father and me, for instance. If we'd succeeded at being careful, we would never have taken a chance on each other."

"You look so innocent for someone who dumped your fiancé to marry his best friend," he teased.

She made a sound that he could easily interpret as *Watch yourself, kid.* "In any case," she said, "I get the sense that Grace has been careful for too long already. She's obviously a very accomplished and determined woman, given that she has a successful freelance writing career and has done a marvelous job of raising her son by herself. If you ask me, there is a daring woman inside of her just itching to bust out."

It was just what he'd seen, too, and was the reason he didn't feel guilty about last night's kiss. Not only because she'd been the one to start it, but also because it was obvious how much she'd *wanted* it.

"I remember what it was like to want something so badly that it scared me, Dylan. Scared me enough that I thought pushing your father away was the only thing that made sense."

He knew his mother was warning him that the route to Grace's heart might not be a smooth one. But stormy seas had never scared him. "Do you know why Mason and I bonded right away?"

"Why?"

"Because we both have great moms."

"You've always made it easy, honey. Now, your brother Adam, on the other hand...I've never seen anyone so immune to falling in love."

"All the more reason that we're going to love watching him get twisted up in knots when it finally happens. Got anyone in mind who'd be capable of turning him into a pretzel?"

His mother made a considering sound. "Actually, now that you mention it, I just might. I need to give Rafe and Brooke a quick ring."

"You've got something up your sleeve, haven't you?"

"Always," she said with a laugh. "Have a good time with Grace and Mason tonight, sweetie."

"I will." He had absolutely no doubt about that. Just as he knew that despite what Grace tried to tell herself about last night's kiss being their one and only, more kisses were definitely on tonight's menu.

* * *

Writing had always been easy for Grace. She'd loved her English classes in high school and college and when other students had been moaning about having to write their essays, she'd focused on fine-tuning hers until they sang. Writing for a newspaper had been intense with tight deadlines that had no room for error, but she'd enjoyed rising to—and meeting— those challenges. Once she'd gone freelance and that career path had gone well, too, she'd assumed that it would always be an enjoyable ride from idea to finished story. Writer's block had been something she hadn't been able to comprehend, not when the words always flowed and the process of putting them down was such an enjoyable one.

Until she got pregnant.

Of all the publications she'd written for, and all the topics she'd covered, amazingly, pregnancy hadn't been anywhere on the list. Which meant the brain fog from rapidly shifting hormones during her first trimester hit her from completely out of the blue. It didn't help, of course, that she'd also been dumped and that her ex's family had tried to pay her off at the exact same time.

The words that had always been right there for the plucking were suddenly *much* harder to find. But she'd had continual deadlines from all the magazines and newspapers that kept accepting her pitches, so she continued to slog through her writing days.

Mason hadn't been a difficult baby, thank God, but without the extra money to pay for child care, she had been fitting her writing in at nap time for the past ten months. Naps that were, she noted as she heard her son carry on a cheerful conversation in baby language with his stuffed giraffe in his crib, getting shorter and shorter all the time. Mason didn't want to waste his time sleeping. He wanted to be out exploring and playing.

Figuring she probably had another fifteen minutes to make a final pass through her story on paying off a mortgage early before Mason insisted she come get him from his crib, she was very glad that by the time she finished her final edit, the words had started to come a little bit faster. Earlier in the week, she'd been struggling to put this piece together so that it read like the fun, energetic article she'd promised the magazine editor. Today, however, for the first time in a year and a half, instead of feeling like she was pulling and yanking the words, she had simply been trying to get them down as fast as they came to her.

She hoped that today would be the beginning of a long string of good, flowing writing days. But had her writing finally started to click again because of the simple passage of time bringing her innate gift back to her? Or were her juices flowing again because of the great evening—and mind-blowing kiss—that she'd shared with Dylan Sullivan yesterday?

Earlier, before Mason had gone down for his afternoon nap, she'd multitasked by playing with her son and transcribing the interview while he was happily absorbed with one of his toys. Mason had looked up when he'd heard Dylan speak and had grinned widely before crawling around the small apartment to look for the man who had clearly already become one of his favorite people. When he couldn't find Dylan and had begun to get upset, she'd distracted him with some Cheerios, then decided to wait until he went down for his nap to finish transcribing so that he wouldn't be so confused about why his new friend was hiding from him.

Some writers hated the transcription process, so much so that they would hire companies to do the work for them. But Grace loved having the chance to pick up on things she hadn't noticed during the actual interview, from a slight nuance in her subject's voice to an important detail. Particularly when she'd been slightly distracted at Dylan's parents' house by hoping that Mason was being good with Claudia...and also by how difficult it had been to turn off her hormones around Dylan. More than difficult, actually.

Pretty much impossible.

Grace tried not to beat herself up too much about that, though. Not when she was certain that even the most hardened journalist would soften around him. Not only because of his good looks and easy charm, but also because his answers were intelligent and insightful. For all that he loved the sea and his boats, he didn't make sailing out to be perfect. On the contrary, he was honest about the dangers, and about the fact that it could be both scary and lonely.

It would be so much easier to guard her heart against Dylan if he were simply a good-looking man who also happened to be a great kisser. Instead, he was surprisingly balanced despite the fact that he could have held the entire world in his hands if he'd wanted to. Olympic medals. World Cup racing wins. And the most beautiful women in the world.

Somehow, she'd need to keep herself from doing anything stupid tonight. Their one sizzling-hot kiss last night had been hard enough on her peace of mind. Especially now that she knew for certain precisely how dangerous the sexual energy simmering just below the surface of Dylan's easy smiles was...and worse still, how every part of her wanted to find out just how exciting and explosive it would be when he lost control.

Mason's conversation with his giraffe was rising in volume by the time she forcibly corralled her X-rated thoughts. She was about to close the screen on her laptop when a picture caught her attention on the news page that had popped up when she opened her email to send the mortgage article to her editor.

Her gut twisted as she looked at a picture of her ex, the woman he'd married a year ago, and the older Bentleys at the White House correspondents' dinner. They looked just as they had a year and a half ago, with no shadows or guilt marring their perfect smiles. No one would look at this picture and believe they had given her money to get rid of her baby. Yet again, the caption of the picture mentioned her ex's issues with infertility, which had been leaked to the press via an unnamed source who was "close to the family."

Her gut twisted with fear again—Mason might have been born out of wedlock, but in the absence of any legitimate children, he was the one and only Bentley heir to their *Fortune* 500 throne! Thank God Dylan had agreed to let her write the cover story about him so that she could put more money toward her just-in-case defense fund. She would *never* let that family take her son away from her. Not in a million years.

A few moments later, a new photo popped up on the screen, and Grace was stunned yet again, not by another picture of her ex, but by one of Smith Sullivan and his beautiful fiancée, Valentina. According to the text beneath the photo, they had also attended the dinner in Washington, D.C.

How close to her ex had Dylan's cousin been? Had they sat at the same table? Were they friends? Did they do business together?

There could have been no more perfect, or potent, reminder of how crazy she'd be if she let one kiss with Dylan sway her. She'd sworn she would never forget to keep her guard up, and yet look how quickly it had started falling.

But it was more than that. What would a Sullivan want with a nearly broke single mother? A year and a half ago, she hadn't wanted to sit down and examine what it was that Richard had wanted from her, what his angle was. She'd simply wanted to be swept away from everything, especially the pain of losing her father. Now, she knew she needed not only to be more careful, but to be smarter, too, rather than just letting herself fall for the fantasy again.

Especially when the fantasy was likely to up and sail away to far-flung lands at any time.

After closing her laptop, she worked to shake off her black mood as she walked into the bedroom. Hearing her approach, Mason grinned and reached out for her.

Her child was the most important thing in her world, and nothing—not even the hottest kiss ever with Dylan Sullivan—would change that.

CHAPTER NINE

Instinct, for a sailor, was much more important than intellect. It wasn't that sailors weren't smart—all those long hours at sea when the winds weren't cooperating made reading anything you could get your hands on crucial to keep from losing your mind sometimes. It was simply that a great sailor understood that analytics and calculations could never be a match for a wild and beautiful ocean that could easily outmatch the best radar and the newest computer consoles.

After the kiss Dylan and Grace had shared the night before, he believed more strongly than ever that the instincts he had been trusting for thirty-one years were going to lead him in the right direction, yet again. And soon, he hoped, Grace would learn to trust her own instincts again, too, even if she had clearly lifted her guard all the way back up in the wake of last night's kiss.

Keeping things light and easy all evening at the aquarium, as friends, would hopefully be the first step to truly earning Grace's heart. Hating that she'd been hurt and felt she needed to be so wary and cautious with him, he silently vowed to do whatever he could to help her learn that it was okay to risk—and to trust him. Still, it wasn't easy to rein in the fierce urge to yank those walls back down by giving her another kiss.

Mason giggled as a group of koi swam, quick and slippery, beneath his little fingertips in the tank. For the past half hour he'd refused to leave this spot.

"I've taken him to aquariums before, but he's never responded like this. Actually being able to touch and feed the animals makes such a huge difference." Grace's eyes were shining with gratitude when she turned to him. "Please thank your friend for agreeing to stay open late so that we could come here tonight. Between Mason's nap times and my trying to fit in work around them, I would never have been able to work it out." Turning back to her son, she said, "It's time to say good-bye to everyone now so that they can close up."

Dylan did his best not to laugh at Mason's stubborn look and the slight shake of his head. No question about it, this kid was going to be a handful one day. Just like Dylan and his siblings had been. Still were, actually, despite his mother having said that he'd made it easy on her. She'd been strict about kindness and manners, but in everything else she'd always just let them be kids. Even if getting wild and stupid had sometimes—usually—resulted in banged-up bones and scraped skin.

He was impressed by how well Grace dealt with what might have turned into a tantrum when she started to wave bye-bye to the fish and Mason got so caught up in mirroring her that he forgot about not wanting to leave.

As soon as they walked away from the tank, Mason reached out for Dylan. But instead of passing him over, Grace gave her son a kiss on the forehead and said, "He's already been carrying you most of the night. You can stay with me for a little while."

"I'm happy to take him, Grace."

"I know you are, but—" She scrunched up her nose, looking as cute as her kid always did. "It's been just the two of us for so long that I guess I'm not yet sure how I feel about him being so comfortable in anyone else's arms. Which really isn't fair when I can see how much he likes being around another guy."

"You're obviously the most important person in the world to him. But if you ever want to lean on someone else for a while, I'm here."

He could tell she wanted to ask him why he was already clearly all-in—especially since asking the important questions was a large part of the reason she'd chosen journalism. At the same time, it wasn't too hard to guess that the reason she didn't was because she wasn't yet ready to hear his answer.

"I've seen how great you are with Mason," she said instead, "but you're also quite a trouper around so many other little kids."

Not all of the children in the aquarium had been as thrilled to be there as Mason was. In fact, Dylan's left ear was still ringing from one girl's high-pitched screams. "I like kids. Even if that one did split a hole in my eardrum."

Grace laughed. "I thank God every day that Mason is so easygoing. Your mom said you were, too."

He raised his eyebrows. "What else did she tell you?"

"We didn't get a chance to talk for very long. Though I wish we had, because I would have liked to know more about your childhood."

He enjoyed seeing her skin flush as she admitted to wanting to know more about him, and he had to forcibly rein in the urge to reach out to stroke its softness. Especially when her eyes met his and he knew that she was thinking exactly the same thing.

* * *

Grace had reminded herself a dozen times that last night's kiss with Dylan had been a one-time aberration. She couldn't repeat it, couldn't give in to the temptation to start anything with him that went beyond her magazine story and maybe becoming friends. But that had been before she'd seen him with Mason again. The two of them had been absolutely adorable together all night, and more than one woman had looked at her with envy when they'd seen Dylan and Mason playing together.

It would have been so easy to let herself pretend that they were actually a family, that Mason had a father who loved him. But Grace knew better, knew that giving in to fantasies like that would only make it harder to go back to being just the two of them. Still, it wasn't at all easy to keep her walls up during one of the most enjoyable evenings out in a very long time.

"I was thinking we could get something to eat nearby," Dylan said, "but Mason is probably going to hit the wall soon, isn't he?"

Her son wasn't giving any indication that he was at all tired—in fact, just the opposite, as being with Dylan had made him more bright-eyed and excited than ever—but Grace knew firsthand just how quickly smiles could change to tears when Mason was overtired. Clearly, Dylan had a sixth sense for kids. Women, too, given how well he'd done with her tonight. He hadn't tried to kiss her, hadn't tried to pressure her in any way into feeling that this was a date. And with nothing to push against, she'd ended up relaxing more and more into the evening.

At this point, her guard had pretty much come down all the way. Which is precisely why she knew she should take the easy out and cut off their evening there. They'd all had fun, and if she and Mason headed home now from their perfectly friendly aquarium trip, there wouldn't be a chance for another kiss like the one she and Dylan had shared last night.

But when she opened her mouth to thank him for a great evening and say good night, what came out instead was, "I could make us something to eat back at my place."

Both Dylan *and* Mason smiled, already two peas in a pod. "Sounds good to me," Dylan said as he gave her son's little hand a high five.

The first thing Grace did when they got back to her apartment was open a bottle of wine and pour them each a glass. Before Dylan could take a sip, Mason crawled over with a toy car in each hand and tugged on his leg.

"You want to race? I was going to help your mommy with dinner, but if you need a playmate..."

She laughed, easily guessing Dylan wasn't much for working in the kitchen. "I'm making the easiest, quickest dinner in history, so I don't need any help. Go play. I hope you like spaghetti and salad."

"Love it." He grinned down at her son. "And I love racing cars, too."

As he went to sit in the middle of the living room rug where Mason gleefully crashed their cars together, she was struck by how easy this was. The one time she'd made dinner for her ex, desperate not to disappoint him, she'd spent days planning the menu and then hours that night putting it all together. And even then, she hadn't gotten the sense he was particularly impressed, not when Michelin-starred chefs were much more his speed. Plus, he'd been far more interested in getting her into bed than in eating dinner together.

Tonight, however, it was really nice to have company while she worked in the kitchen, listening to Mason and Dylan drive toy cars on the living room floor.

When Mason crawled off to gather up more cars to share with his new best friend, Dylan asked, "When did you decide you wanted to be a writer?"

"To be honest, I don't think I really gave anything else a chance. I always loved to read anything I could get my hands on, and English was my favorite subject at school."

"You probably turned in your book reports early, didn't you?"

"I know, I was a weird kid," she said with a laugh. "What about you? What was your favorite class?"

"Summer."

She couldn't remember the last time she'd laughed so much in one night. "After that? No," she said as she turned from the stove, "let me guess. Physics. Math, probably, too. Because both subjects would help you make sense of the way a boat moves and how it's put together."

Dylan reached for Mason and pulled him onto his lap. "Your mommy knows stuff, kid.

Which means you're never going to get away with anything." Mason was rubbing his eyes and yawning as Dylan stood up with him. "You're one hell of a writer, Grace."

She was plating their spaghetti and nearly spilled it onto the counter in her surprise. "You've read my work?"

"I'm not surprised you won an award for your coverage of that huge earthquake in Chile a few years back. Your love for writing well-researched and compassionate stories comes through on every page."

Her flush, she decided, could be explained by standing over a hot stove, although they both knew it had far more to do with how much his compliment meant to her.

"Thanks." She brought their plates over to the table. "I can take him while we eat."

"We're good," Dylan said, making it seem like the most natural thing to eat his dinner with a ten-month-old on his lap, just as he had last night at his parents' house.

"He's usually already sacked out by this time in the evening. I think he was just so excited by having you here that he wanted to squeeze every ounce of playtime out of you."

"I know exactly how he feels," Dylan said as Mason nuzzled his head closer against his shoulder and closed his eyes. He looked up from her son, his gaze quickly shifting from affection for the baby to heat for her. "It's been a good night, hasn't it?"

"It has." She made herself pick up her fork and twirl spaghetti onto it even though she didn't think she'd be able to eat much with Dylan so close...and so *male*. "It's nice having a friend to spend time with."

She half-expected him to point out that by now they had clearly transitioned from just friends. But Dylan, she was learning, rarely did what people expected him to. So after telling her that her spaghetti dinner might very well rival his Aunt Mary's, he said, "Tell me about your folks."

She couldn't stop the rush of anguish. "They're both gone."

He put his fork down and reached across the table to cover her hand. "I'm sorry."

"I am, too." The warmth, the strength of his hand over hers helped to ground her. "My mother got sick with lung cancer when I was in elementary school. She had never smoked, but her father had been a heavy smoker during her childhood. My father and I, we were both devastated, but he never missed a beat. He was there for me every single second. We had always been close, but we became an even tighter unit after my mom died." She turned her hand palm up so that she could grip Dylan's. "Two years ago, he was coming home from a baseball game when someone who had been drinking heavily at the same game drove through a red light. The paramedics said he died instantly, that he probably felt no pain." But she had. Pain that could still spear her from out of the blue. "I miss him every day, so much, just the way I still miss my mom. But never more than when Mason does something new, like his first smile, or when he started to crawl. My father, my mother—they will never get to see those things. And Mason will never get to know his grandparents."

She didn't know when Dylan moved close enough to pull her against him so that the baby was leaning against one broad shoulder and she was in the crook of the other.

"They raised one hell of a woman, Grace. And you're doing just as great a job with Mason."

"He looks like my father. The same eyes. The same silly grin."

Mason blinked bleary eyes open and reached for her then, and she knew she was going to pay the next morning for keeping him up so far past his bedtime, but she hadn't wanted the evening with Dylan to end, either. Not when it truly had been a perfect night.

So perfect that she didn't think she could live with herself if she didn't explain precisely why she was so intent on them being "just friends" after a kiss that had proved they could be so much more.

"I know we've only just started to eat, but I need to put Mason to bed. But, please, stay and finish dinner. And if you wouldn't mind staying a little longer, I'd like to answer the question you asked me last night."

"Of course I'll wait, Grace. As long as you need me to." He gave Mason a kiss on the forehead. "Good night, little guy. Sweet dreams."

Mason's eyes fluttered open again, and when he puckered up his lips to give Dylan a good-night kiss—something he'd only ever given her before tonight—Grace's heart flip-flopped inside her chest.

From the look on Dylan's face, she knew his had, too.

CHAPTER TEN

Regardless of how difficult or crazy a day Grace might have had, Mason's bedtime ritual always settled her down. Tonight, however, she had a feeling nothing was going to stop the flutters in her belly. Because even though she was about to tell Dylan about her past so that he'd understand why she couldn't date him, it didn't change the fact that she was still going to be alone in her living room with the sexiest man alive.

She resisted the urge to fix her hair or makeup before going back out to see him, just as she hadn't allowed herself to stress over her outfit. Jeans and a T-shirt had been perfect for a visit to the aquarium, and they would still be perfect for an honest discussion between friends.

She was surprised to find that Dylan had cleaned up the dining room and kitchen. "You didn't have to do that."

"You've met my mother, so you should know that no Sullivan ever shirks on cleanup. Are you sure you don't want me to heat yours back up?"

She shook her head, but picked up her glass of wine before going to sit on the couch. As soon as he sat beside her, she said, "Last night, you asked me why I didn't want to date you. I know it sounds like a cliché, but it's not you, it's me. I met Mason's—" She shook her head, unable to use the word *father*. Not when Richard had never been, not for one single second. "I was researching a story about charitable foundations. He is one of the leading experts in family-run charities because he comes from an influential Washington family with legacy money." The irony still killed her that the family everyone thought was so good, so charitable, had been anything but when they'd learned she was pregnant. "I thought that just because he spent his days giving away money, it meant he was a good person, too. So even though I know how to do really good background research on people, I let the fact that he worked for an organization that helps people in need take the place of actually looking deeper." She wasn't proud of it, but she needed Dylan to know something else. "He was so good at sweeping me off my feet, taking me on his private plane and to rooftop dinners just for the two of us that after things ended with him, I swore I wouldn't let that happen to me again—falling for a pretty face and slick words just because I might be feeling lonely."

"I'm glad you think my face is pretty," Dylan said with a small upturn of his lips, "but nothing I've said to you has been slick."

She wanted to believe him, wished it was easy for her to take all the nice things he'd said at face value. "I was never one of those daughters who had to rebel. But once my parents were both gone, I felt so lost—" She stopped herself. "It sounds like I'm making an excuse for what I did, for the choices I made."

"No, it sounds like you're human. Like you were hurting and needed someone to comfort you. But he hurt you instead." Anger flashed in Dylan's eyes. "What did he do when you told him you were pregnant?"

She hadn't been planning to go into the nitty-gritty details tonight. Even though she hadn't given any names, she'd probably already said too much. But after having a glass of wine on an empty stomach, she couldn't seem to stop. Especially not when Dylan was such a good listener...and the only person she'd ever told about any of this.

"He acted like I'd tricked him. Like I'd done it on purpose to get his money, to force his hand to marry me so that I could live off his family fortune."

"How could he not know how much you love your work, and that you would never do something like that? That you could never even have it in you to think of it?"

"Probably because he didn't care about what I did. He didn't respect my career, or me, either. I would never in a million years want to become a kept woman. Never. But since he didn't believe that, he told me my trick of getting pregnant wasn't going to work. When I swore to him that it was an accident, that he knew we had used protection, he didn't want to listen. And he told me..." Her stomach twisted. "He told me to undo it."

Dylan's curse was soft, but powerful nonetheless. "The bastard didn't deserve you."

"I know he didn't. I think I knew it long before that night, actually. We were always alone, just the two of us on a yacht or in a fancy hotel suite or my apartment. I thought it was because he wanted to get to know me better before he introduced me to his friends and family. But what he was really doing was hiding me from them and from the other woman he was actually going to marry—one who was infinitely more appropriate in his world. But I didn't want to be alone, so I didn't stop seeing him even though I should have."

She paused, took another sip of wine to try to steady herself. But it was no use. Not when she had an even worse part of the story to tell.

"I was still reeling from his reaction the next day—and trying to wrap my head around having a baby on my own—when I had a couple of unexpected visitors. His parents didn't want to risk leaving anything to chance. And, I think they were used to cleaning up their son's messes over the years by throwing money at them. They gave me the money and tried to act like it was a gift. But I made them tell me, made them say aloud what it was for. They expected me to get rid of Mason and forget I'd ever had anything to do with their son."

"Tell me his name, Grace."

She knew she shouldn't, but since she'd already been crazy enough to tell Dylan this much—more than she'd ever intended to tell anyone—it wouldn't be hard for him to put the pieces together. "Richard. Richard Bentley."

His eyebrows went up with surprise even as his gaze simmered with obvious fury. "The former senator and his wife gave you money and told you and your baby to disappear?"

"That's why I left Washington. Not because they paid me to—I didn't cash their checks—but because I couldn't risk letting them or Richard see that I'd decided to have the baby."

"Do they know where you are?"

"No. At least, I don't think they do." She tried to keep the rest from spilling out, but couldn't. "Richard is having trouble conceiving with his new wife. I've seen a couple of news reports online about it this week. Before now, I was pretty positive that Richard and his family thought I was so insignificant, and so lacking in strength, that they wouldn't bother trying to track me down once I'd left Washington. Especially given that they'd told me that if I tried to say a word against them, their charity—one that helps disadvantaged women, ironically— would be what people sided with. Not a woman who had clearly gotten knocked up on purpose to try to lock their son into marrying her to set her up for life." She took a shaky breath. "But now that I know Richard might not be able to have the Bentley heir they were all expecting his wife to give them..."

"I can help you, Grace. I can help keep you and Mason safe from them."

She gave him a small smile to let him know she appreciated his offer even if she couldn't possibly take him up on it. God, she could only imagine what a mess *that* would be, especially since she'd seen for herself that afternoon that at least one of Dylan's cousins ran in the same circles as the Bentleys. Dylan's family had been nothing but nice to her and Mason. She wouldn't drag them into her mess.

"When you were talking about sailing through a storm during our interview, I realized that I've been there. Finding out that I was pregnant and then realizing that I was going to have to be a parent all by myself has been one of the most frightening things I've ever done, but also one of the most beautiful. My parents raised me to be strong, but I was never really tested before and never knew what I was capable of. Or how tough I could really be. Now I do, and I have a plan for how to fight them just in case I ever need to. But thank you for offering to help us. Honestly, it's enough that you agreed to do this story with me. That already helps a great deal."

"You're so damned strong, Grace, that anyone who can't see it is a total idiot." Had anyone ever looked at her with such respect and admiration? "But my brother Rafe is a P.I. And Ian is one of the wealthiest men in the world, with business ties to pretty much everyone. My brothers can help make sure nothing ever happens to you and Mason. Let me talk to them. Let us make absolutely sure that your ex and his family aren't up to anything." He took her hand in his. "I promise you that they'll stay totally below the radar. They won't stir anything up."

It was so overwhelming, the way he was offering to help in any way he could to keep her and her son safe. "But we—"

She stopped herself before she could protest that they'd only just met. What did it matter how long she'd known Dylan when he was offering to do whatever he and his family could to keep her son safely with her?

"Yes," she finally said. "Okay."

"You'll let us help?"

Utterly overwhelmed with emotion from all sides, she nodded. "I'd appreciate it, actually, not having everything fall on me for once."

"Thank you for trusting me not only to help, but also by telling me about your past."

"I couldn't let you think there was something wrong with you." Realizing that sounded strange, she quickly added, "I mean, obviously you've looked in a mirror, so you know that's not the problem." Ugh, that only made things worse, even though he'd smiled when she said it. "It's just now that you know where I am in my life and where I've come from, you can understand why I promised myself that I wouldn't make that same mistake again. I can't jump into a relationship right now and don't honestly know when or if I'll be able to again. Not now that everything inside of me has shut down."

"Shut down?" He shook his head. "There was nothing shut down about the kiss we shared last night."

She knew he was right. There was no point trying to deny it, even if a part of her argument fell apart. "You're right," she said, "there wasn't. But one kiss doesn't change anything."

Grace had spent enough time with Dylan in the past two days to know how to read the look in his eyes. Instinct was vitally important to him, but that didn't mean he wouldn't take time to think things through. Right now, he was processing everything she'd said.

"After what you've been through," he finally said, "I can understand how hard it must be to trust anyone. Especially another man."

She was surprised—very surprised, actually—that what she'd said seemed to be enough to make him back down from wanting to date her. It was what she'd told herself she wanted, and yet...

"Good," she made herself say. "I'm glad you understand."

"After what that scumbag and his family did to you, anyone would be wary and want to take things slow the next time."

She was with him right up until the end...when he got to *slow* and *next time*. "Dylan—"

"If slow is what you need, I can do slow."

She knew she shouldn't let excitement flood back through her. Shouldn't let it push all of the earlier disappointment aside. Especially since Dylan was a champion racer and she doubted there was even a trace of *slow* in his blood.

Then again, building wooden sailboats by hand was perhaps one of the most painstaking careers he could have chosen. *Maybe he could make a promise to go slow and mean it.*

Still, she couldn't just give in like this, could she? Couldn't let a simple promise that he would go slow be enough to change her mind about everything she'd been so certain about for so long. She needed to be rational. Strong.

"In the past two days, I've met your entire family and have spent two consecutive evenings with you. If that's your version of slow, we both know it's not a good idea."

"That's not even close to my entire family," he corrected with a grin before sobering again.

"I know I've pushed you. It's just—" She knew from the way he was looking at her, his eyes so dark, so intense, that she didn't have a prayer of being prepared for whatever he was going to say next. "I saw you and I knew."

"You *knew?*" She could feel her breath coming faster as she watched the shift happen inside Dylan—from thinking and processing to pure male instinct. She felt as she imagined a lioness would when her mate found her. Hunted—and just as suddenly hungry for him as he was for her. "What did you know?"

He reached for her then, the barest brush of his fingertips across her cheek enough to send her heart leaping and racing. "I knew this." She watched him watch her, and when she didn't pull away—Lord, how could she?—he slowly drew his fingers down to the nape of her neck. "I knew your skin would be this soft, this sensitive." Thrill bumps rose all over her body as he ran his fingertips down from her neck over her T-shirt, then to the bare skin of her arm exposed by the short sleeve. "I knew you'd be this responsive." Somewhere in there, she reached for him without even realizing it so that her hands were holding on to his waist. "I knew we would fit together this perfectly."

Grace knew she should find more words, more reasons that she couldn't do this, but she really, *really* didn't want to. Not when it had been so long since she'd felt sensual pleasure. And not when it seemed like forever since she'd felt even the least bit feminine or had thought about anything but her son and her work.

She didn't see how this could last, how it could turn into something real—how the gorgeous, incredible man from the amazing and famous family could ever look at a normal woman with a ten-month-old child and see a future. But, hadn't she waited so long to feel this way? Not just a year and a half, but her entire life? For a man who made her want like this, who made her crave with every last fiber of her being?

Last night, she'd let herself have a taste. One perfect, wonderful taste of Dylan. Why couldn't she have one more? Especially when he was right that she was only human.

Too human to know how to keep resisting him tonight...

CHAPTER ELEVEN

"I want to kiss you, Grace. I've wanted to kiss you a hundred times tonight. Every time you smile. Every time you laugh. Every time your body brushes up against mine."

It would have been easiest for both of them if he simply took what he wanted by leaning in and taking that kiss. One kiss without her permission and their incredible chemistry would take over.

But he hadn't made it easy on her from the first, and she knew he wouldn't cop to doing that now. *What do you want?* was what he was asking her. And he was waiting for her answer with the patience that he must have honed from hours working in his boathouse building beautiful boats with his magical hands and brain.

Grace wasn't nearly as patient, though. "I've wanted to kiss you, too, all those times."

She didn't know who moved first tonight, but it didn't matter. All that mattered was how sweet it was to let pleasure sizzle through her as their lips touched. All night long, they'd been leading up to this. To this kiss. To his hands on her and hers on him. She knew that now—finally accepted it as inevitable.

Kissing Dylan wasn't about weakness, wasn't about not having enough self-control. On the contrary, it was about being strong enough to let herself have what she wanted.

What she *needed*.

Her heart jumped in her chest and she lost her breath as he loved her mouth so tenderly. So seductively. Locking her arms around his neck, she all but melted against him, and knew from the low groan he gave just how much he liked having her pliant and aroused against him.

"Soft." He pressed a kiss to the corner of her mouth, and then more down across her cheek. "You're so soft." She lifted her chin so that he could nibble at the underside of her jaw. "You smell so good." He ran his lips down the sensitive skin of her neck, nibbling at her between kisses. "You taste so sweet." His hands were warm on the small of her back, warmer still as he slipped them just beneath the fabric to rest on her bare skin. But instead of taking the next step and pulling her shirt off over her head, he said, "Tell me to stop and I'll stop."

She loved that he was a man of such deep contrasts. So sweet, so gentle...and yet so full of passion and desire. Desire that she could feel him barely holding back, barely controlling.

All because he wanted her with the same ferocity as she wanted him.

"Don't stop. Please don't stop."

Grace felt hot and tingly beneath her clothes. And from the first moment she'd seen him, she'd wondered about what he had beneath his. Any woman with a beating heart would have. Now was her chance to stop wondering and find out.

Forcibly pushing away any lingering thoughts that she was forgetting all of her hard-won lessons and the vows she'd made not to repeat her mistakes, she reached for the hem of his shirt and quickly pulled it up. He was more than happy to help, drawing back and lifting his arms so that she could take it all the way off.

Grace obviously wasn't a virgin. Not even close, if that slightly wild year she'd had back in college counted. But...oh my...there wasn't a man alive who could have prepared her for the way Dylan Sullivan looked without his shirt. Tanned and muscular. Lean and honed from daily sails and woodworking.

Perfect.

She didn't think, couldn't think anymore, could only lay her hands flat on his chest. His skin was so warm and his muscles jumped beneath her fingertips as she explored his incredible male beauty. She was a terrible painter—putting words together was the only art she'd ever been good at—but if she could draw, she'd want him to model for her.

But it wasn't enough just to look, to touch. She had to put her mouth on him, too. Her lips had only just touched his shoulder when a low, rough sound rumbled from his chest. She barely had a chance to slick her tongue against him when she found herself lying back against the arm of her couch with Dylan's hands in her hair and his kisses stealing her breath.

Every taste she took of him, instead of sating her the way she'd expected, only made her more ravenous. Every kiss they shared only made her want more. More of his tongue tangling with hers. More of his teeth nipping into her lower lip. More of his heady need for her.

She'd been wanted before, but never like this. And never by a man so beautifully put together or so in tune with how to give a woman pleasure. It was perfectly natural to fall deeper and deeper into his kiss, and to relish how good his hands, big and rough from working with wood and rope and tools all day, felt moving over her skin. The way he was gentle and yet powerful all at the same time—barely skirting that edge of control—made Grace melt into his touch.

Loving the heavy weight of his body over hers, she instinctively wrapped her arms around him and pulled him closer. She wanted more.

More. *More.* But then, suddenly, she felt him shift farther away, rather than closer.

As she blinked up at him through eyes gone blurry with lust, while he ran his hands over her face, shoulders, and then the full lengths of her arms until he reached her hands, where he threaded their fingers together, she thought she knew why. Dylan wasn't stopping because he didn't want her. She could see, could feel, just how much he did.

The reason he'd reined them both in was because he was afraid of pushing her too far.

Because he *cared.*

He could easily have continued to seduce her with kisses and caresses until she was too mindless to be able to think at all. Until she wasn't able to make choices, only soak in sensation. Until it was too late for her to realize that they were crossing the line between feeling blissfully alive and feeling regretful.

But the truth was that stopping here, stopping now, when they hadn't gone any further than two teenagers necking on the couch—that was something she'd *definitely* regret. Especially if this was her one and only chance to allow herself the wonder of Dylan's touch.

She didn't want to break the sexy spell, but she needed to be completely honest with him right now, or moving forward wouldn't feel right for either of them.

"I can't have sex with you tonight." Because for as good as it would be, and she had no doubt that her body would rejoice, her mind and heart weren't even close to being ready for such intimacy. "I don't know when I'll be ready for that again. But—" She licked her lips, watched his hungry gaze shift momentarily to her mouth before they locked on her eyes again. "I do want this. I want you. I want your body against mine. I want your mouth, your hands on me. I want—"

It was scary to say all of these things, scary to even think them after she'd put herself into a safe freeze for so long. But Grace knew with utter certainty that it would be far worse to turn back rather than take a risk. And no matter what happened after tonight, if they decided to keep slowly moving forward or agreed to step all the way back from each other instead, she refused to regret rediscovering pleasure. Rediscovering *herself.* Not when she'd only just realized that here was yet another thing her ex had tried to take from her—her confidence in her natural sensuality, her healthy feminine responses to being touched, kissed, wanted.

She wouldn't let her ex keep taking that from her. *Couldn't* let him.

"I want to feel like a woman again, Dylan. I want to remember what it's like to feel sexy. To be desired. To let myself go, even just a little bit, for a little while. And I want to go there with *you.*"

She had barely finished speaking when his mouth covered hers again. In his kiss—one so sweet, yet dangerously sexy all at the same time—she felt his promise to give her everything she needed.

* * *

For all that Dylan loved his boats and the ocean, women had always trumped both. He loved hearing a woman laugh. Loved seeing the flash of fire in a strong woman's eyes. But nothing he'd ever experienced came close to how good it felt to have Grace in his arms, her heart racing in time with his, her mouth sweetly seductive against his as they kissed.

He'd wanted her at first glance. He'd liked her as soon as she'd stood in his boathouse and tried to persuade him to do the interview. And now, from nothing more than a handful of minutes making out with her on her living room couch, he knew that he'd crave her for the rest of his life.

Their hands were still linked as she slid his beneath her shirt, over the soft skin of her stomach, past her rib cage, finally stopping at her bra. "Touch me," she breathed against his mouth barely a beat before she laid his hands over her full breasts. "I need you to touch me."

He could feel the heat of her through smooth silk and only barely restrained himself from tearing it from her. Her nipples were hard against his palms, and though he tried to be gentle, he couldn't control the urge to stroke, to tease.

She felt like heaven, but it wasn't enough just to touch. He needed to see, too. "I want to touch all of you."

She didn't hesitate to reach for the hem of her T-shirt. But he had one hell of a fantasy that he was dying to see come true. So he moved his hands to hers again and lifted them to his mouth for a kiss before setting them above her head.

"I want you to hold still for me and let me have the pleasure of undressing you. Can you do that for me?"

Her eyes widened, and he watched her throat move before she answered. "*Yes.*"

It was, he found himself thinking, like unwrapping a much-longed-for gift. He was torn between tearing off her shirt or drawing it out slowly to savor the anticipation. Overpowering desire made the decision for him, and seconds later her T-shirt was on the living room rug next to his.

Lying before him wearing only a simple white silk bra, she stole his breath. "You're beautiful, Grace."

"I've always been curvy," she said in a soft voice as she looked down to follow the path of his tanned hands up over her rib cage until he was barely stroking the undersides of her breasts through silk. "But since I had Mason I'm even curvier."

"Yet another reason to love that kid," he murmured as he shifted his palms to fully cup her. "Your body, your breasts, every part of you is perfect."

"I haven't been with anyone in a long time. Not since I found out I was pregnant."

It meant more to Dylan than she would ever know that she was trusting him to be with her, not only since having Mason, but also since being so horribly betrayed. He felt the weight, the responsibility, of earning her trust, even as he gave silent thanks to the universe that he was being given this chance to prove that he was worthy of her.

Even if he couldn't find the right words to persuade her to see just how beautiful she was, he could do it with a kiss. Slowly, as he loved her mouth with his own, he felt her relax again beneath him and knew right when she forgot to be shy because she twined her arms around his neck and arched up into him.

It was a crime for Grace to believe, for any reason, that she was "shut down." All Dylan wanted tonight was to make her feel good. So good that she'd never be able to question her innate sensuality again.

Of course he wanted to protect her. Of course he would never do anything to harm her. But at the same time, he respected her too much to treat her like porcelain. Grace had already proved again and again that she wasn't breakable.

Remembering the way her breath had gone shallow and her pupils had dilated when he'd asked her to keep her hands above her head while he undressed her, he lifted his mouth from hers. "It's time to move your hands back over your head."

Again, her breath quickened and her eyes darkened. He could read the thoughts that crossed her beautiful face: Did she dare trust him? Not only with being her first after such a long drought...but with *this?*

But then, just as he'd expected, the brave and determined expression that he'd already come to know so well returned. Slowly—and so seductively that he knew it didn't matter who was giving the sensual commands, she would always be the one in charge—she untwined her hands from around his neck and lifted them back up to the arm of the couch.

"Whenever I touch you, your skin flushes," he murmured as he grazed his fingertips over her, teasing both of them. "Did you know that?"

Watching the path of his hands over her, she said in a slightly breathless voice, "All you have to do is *look* at me and I heat up all over."

He had to kiss her again, then, so that she'd know how much he liked hearing it. Knowing it.

"It's the same for me," he told her, shifting just enough so that she could feel how much he wanted her. How hot, how fast his blood was pumping, all for her. "You have no idea. No idea how much I want you."

"Then show me, Dylan. Please, show me *now.*"

CHAPTER TWELVE

Permission granted, Dylan didn't let himself overthink his instincts or his fierce need for her—he simply took two handfuls of silk and tore. But in the end, she wasn't the one left most stunned, he was...by the most perfect breasts he'd ever seen.

His hands beat his mouth to her by a split second, and then he was touching, stroking, kissing, licking. First at the sweet, soft flesh, and then the hardened tips again and again and again. He was starved for her, desperate for more, filled with a hunger that was like nothing he'd ever known.

Grace moaned his name as she arched her back so that he could have more of her. He had her jeans off within seconds and would have torn her panties in two just as he'd shredded her bra if he hadn't needed to stop to take a mental picture of how pretty she looked. He covered the damp silk between her legs with his hand

and let out a low curse as he realized how hot, how ready she was.

"Don't stop," she urged him. "Please don't stop now. I need you to touch me, Dylan. I need it so badly. I've never needed like this. *Never.*"

"Neither have I." It was the honest-to-God truth. Watching, feeling Grace come apart was going to *destroy* him.

Dylan was torn again between teasing and taking. But he also knew that the higher he took her before he let her go, the better she would feel, so he forced himself to shove back the animalistic urges that she stirred up in a way no one else ever had, and sway back toward building anticipation. So instead of shredding her panties, he stroked her through them instead.

"Dylan—" He loved hearing her breath hitch. "Oh God...just like that. Keep touching me just like that."

She was gripping the arm of the couch behind her for dear life as she worked to push herself even harder against him, and it was hands-down the sexiest thing Dylan had ever seen in his life. Watching her get herself off against him, still wearing her panties, her full breasts bouncing with every breath, he grew so hard beneath the zipper of his jeans that he figured it would bust open soon.

She'd obviously loved it when he'd had her keep her hands above her head. Something told him a little dirty talk would go over just as well.

"Come for me, Grace. Just like this, riding my hand. Let me see how beautiful you are when you let me help take you over the edge."

Her lids finally fluttered shut, the wet lips she'd been licking opened slightly, and her body bowed in sweet surrender to pleasure.

Dylan had never seen anything so mind-blowingly beautiful in all his life as Grace shuddering against him in climax. How he'd gotten lucky enough to be the guy here with her, the guy she was trusting to give pleasure back to her, he'd never know. All he knew was that he would be thankful for it forever.

He didn't wait for her to come down, couldn't wait one more second to touch—and taste—her bare, wet, heated skin. Silently vowing to buy her new silk to replace this set, the animal inside of him finally came completely unleashed as he tore her panties off.

When he found her with his lips and tongue, she made a sound that he thought might have been his name, but he could barely hear over the roar of his pounding heartbeat in his ears. Where she'd been on the verge of going soft and boneless at the end of her first climax, as soon as he flicked his tongue over her, Dylan could feel her begin to rise again. Maybe it was too much to ask for tonight—for her to come out of a cold front straight into the burning heat of multiple orgasms—but Lord, he wanted it.

Wanted it for both of them.

"Again," he urged her as he slicked his fingers, first one, then another, into her. "I need to feel you let go again, Grace."

He looked up her body as he played over her with his hands, one between her thighs, the other on her luscious breasts, and nearly lost it when he saw how close she was to giving him another sweet release. She wasn't fighting him, wasn't fighting herself. On the contrary, it was just as she'd said and just as he'd hoped: She was reclaiming her sensuality by letting herself go with him tonight, straight to the edge of the limits she'd set just a little while ago. Limits he would never disrespect no matter how badly he wanted her. He would never hurt her. *Never.*

Dylan lowered his mouth back to her sweet skin at the same time as he thrust two fingers in. He curled them against her sensitive inner flesh just as she shattered, her muscles gripping tightly at his fingers as she rocked into his hand again and again.

After, he kissed the insides of both thighs, then made his way slowly back up her body while she worked to catch her breath. "That was..."

She broke off when he ran his hands up the lengths of her arms and threaded his fingers back through hers. He loved how soft, how relaxed she looked now as she blinked up at him.

"I'm a writer. I'm supposed to have words for the way you just made me feel. But I don't."

"You just did," he told her right before he leaned in to kiss her, gentle again despite the unquenched fire raging in his blood. "And I'm right there with you, completely stunned and speechless by how beautiful you are."

So beautiful, and so trusting, that he knew he needed to do the most difficult thing in the world.

"I should go." He kissed her again. "Soon." One more kiss and he forced himself to draw all the way back, bringing her up with him, naked and soft in his arms. "Now."

"But you haven't—"

He kissed her again before she could tear away the very thin thread of control he was still managing to hold on to. "And I won't. Not tonight. Not until you're ready for more."

"I'm still not ready to have sex," she said softly. "But that doesn't mean you need to leave right now. So soon. Not before I touch you, too."

He was tempted. So damned tempted that his hands shook as he picked up the blanket from the other arm of the couch and wrapped it around her. "When I said I want you more than I've ever wanted anyone else, I meant it. That's why I'm not going to stay. Not tonight. Not until you can swear to me without even the slightest hesitation that you're ready for more. Because when that day comes, you'd better believe I'm not going to walk away. Or stop. Not until both of us are so overfull with pleasure, with each other, that we'll be raising the white flag together."

"Thank you," she said softly as she tucked the blanket more tightly around herself, then ran a hand through the hair he'd so enjoyed tangling in his hands as he'd kissed her. "Not only for a great night, start to finish, but also for leaving when it would be so much easier not to."

They both stood, then, her bare feet peeking out from beneath the soft red blanket. What a beauty she was. And what a fool her ex had been not to love her.

He brushed his fingers across her cheek one last time, letting the pad of his thumb linger on her lush lower lip. "Sweet dreams, Grace."

He had barely taken a step back when she surprised the hell out of him by gripping his T-shirt in her fist and yanking him into her. Her kiss was hot and hungry and just as sweet as their first kiss had been the night before, but full of a newfound confidence. The confidence he knew she must have possessed before the rich asshole from D.C. had done everything he could to stomp both her heart, and her life, to bits.

* * *

Dylan knew he couldn't push Grace too hard, or too fast, but making himself walk away when he wanted her more than he'd ever wanted anyone, or anything, in his entire life was one of the hardest things he'd ever done. He'd loved seeing her blurry and needy and knowing it was because of his kisses, his caresses. But the high of her taste, her scent, the sweet little sounds she'd made as he teased her over the edge not just once but twice—none of those things could make him forget his fury at her ex or his worry that one of the Bentleys would come back one day to hurt Grace and Mason.

Dylan's life had been a good one. He didn't have any major demons, any serious darkness in his past, or inner conflicts that kept him tossing and turning at night.

Not until now.

Because he had *her* demons now.

He had never been a violent man. Ian, Rafe, and Adam had always been far more likely to use their fists. But for the first time ever, Dylan could barely think past the urge to track down the bastard who had hurt her and pound the guy's face in.

He pulled out his cell phone as he slid behind the steering wheel and pulled his brothers into a group text.

NEED TO MEET ABOUT KEEPING GRACE AND MASON SAFE.

MY HOUSE. TONIGHT.

By the time he pulled into his garage, his brothers had dropped everything, just as he'd known they would, and were waiting for him.

"Tell us what's going on," Ian said.

Dylan let them inside, poured them all drinks, and pounded his before answering. "What do you know about the Bentleys in D.C.?"

"*Fortune* 500. Generations of money and charity work. Politics."

Dylan downed another shot of whiskey in one gulp. "You can add something else to that list—scum. The guy who got Grace pregnant is a Bentley. But that's not all they did."

Adam leaned in, his expression hard. "What did they do to her?"

"They tried to break her, tried to pay her off to get rid of Mason, and to stay quiet about having anything to do with them."

"The former senator is Mason's father?" Rafe asked incredulously.

"No. The son. Richard Bentley. He accused her of trying to trick him into marriage." He scowled. "As if anyone would actually want to marry into that sick and twisted family."

Ian looked as furious as Dylan felt. "The bastard always seemed too slick."

"The cleaner they seem on the surface," Rafe agreed through his own clenched teeth, "the dirtier they always are underneath. What other details do you have?"

"Richard's parents paid her a visit the day after she gave him the news and shoved their sin money at her while informing her that if she ever tried to go up against them, they'd use their name and charity and connections to crush her." Adam cursed low and long as Dylan laid it all out for his brothers. "She didn't use a dime of their money, didn't want anything to do with them. It's why she left D.C. So that they wouldn't see that she had the baby, and so they wouldn't try to hurt either her or Mason. She doesn't think of Richard as the father. Not after what he and his family did." Dylan's blood was boiling. "Best case, she wants to believe she's hidden and forgotten, but a family like that, they keep tabs on their mistakes. And they think they deserve anything. Everything they want. Whether they should have it or not. Especially now that the word on the street is that her ex and his new wife are having trouble conceiving. What if Richard and his family realize that Mason is the only Bentley heir they're going to have? They'll come after her to try to steal him away." He swore. "I can't just sit on the sidelines. I have to protect her and Mason. I can't risk something happening to them." Before Rafe could ask, he added, "She and I talked tonight about my pulling you guys in. Even though I know she wishes she could handle this situation all by herself, she'll do anything to keep her son safe."

"I'll dig into the guy," Rafe said. "His family, too. Whatever dirt there is on them, I'll find it."

"I'll do the same on the business end," Ian told him. "I'll find out what else the family has their hands in." *And figure out where to yank to destroy them,* was his unspoken promise. "I'll also check in with Smith to see what he knows about the Bentleys."

"And I'll be in charge of keeping you from doing something stupid," Adam said. "I know you're furious. We all are. But right now you need to let Rafe and Ian see what they can dig up, and be there for Grace and Mason. Because going after the bastard and his family now, without any intel or a plan, will likely only raise questions we don't want the Bentleys asking about Grace or a baby they might not know anything about otherwise."

Dylan appreciated the support of his brothers—it was why he'd called them together, because they'd always worked best as a team. And yet, even though he knew he shouldn't head to D.C. and flatten all three of the Bentleys, he hated having to wait, hated having to be patient until they had more information. He had always been able to change what needed to be changed in his life, to fix what needed to be fixed. Sure, he was sometimes frustrated, or angry on his family's behalf for things that had happened to them, but he also knew that whenever they needed help, they'd ask for it because they knew he would always be there for them.

Tonight was the first time Dylan had ever really struggled with the horrible futility of knowing that he couldn't just make the darkness in Grace's past go away.

"Since we can all see that Grace and Mason are already yours," Ian told him, "that means they're ours, too. So if her ex or his family try anything, you can count on all of us to take them down."

CHAPTER THIRTEEN

Grace had spent the last thirty-six hours thinking. Mulling. Dissecting.

And wanting. Always *wanting*.

Saturday night, she'd told Dylan more than she'd ever told anyone else about her past...and then she'd gone a little crazy in his arms. The best kind of crazy, she thought as she pulled into the parking lot of his boathouse. But crazy nonetheless. She'd hoped to have a firm handle on everything by now, but the truth was that she was still going around and around in her mind.

She'd intended for the night to be nothing more than friends visiting an aquarium. But there was no point in trying to deny how good—or how natural—it had been to make out with Dylan on her couch, so she wouldn't bother with that nonsense. She also wouldn't try to tell herself that she hadn't wanted more of his big, work-roughened hands on her. Not when she had wanted *much* more. But he hadn't given her what she was all but begging for, hadn't pushed her too far. Instead, he'd stopped and gone home completely unfulfilled.

Dylan had promised that they would go slow. Given his behavior on Saturday night, it looked as though he meant it. Which was why all her thinking, all her wanting, had her circling back again and again to the same place: If they truly could keep to *slow* while she also kept her eyes wide open this time, then maybe it would be okay to spend a few sexy hours here and there with him.

Attraction, orgasms—they were perfectly natural. And when they were with Dylan, they were perfectly *perfect,* too.

In any case, it wasn't as if making out with him meant they were getting married. A few kisses, a few incredible orgasms, didn't mean forever. Normal people kissed, touched each other. And the truth was that she was tired of fighting her own demons all the time, tired of taking every step with caution, tired of feeling she was going to have to keep paying forever for her mistake with Richard.

Just for a little while, while she and Dylan were working together on this magazine story, couldn't she live a little? Have some fun, feel some pleasure like any other normal woman would let herself feel with a sexy man like him?

She'd been stunned by the way he had shifted from the gentle man he always was during the day with her and Mason to a hungry, dominant lover Saturday night. Stunned in the best possible way, she thought, as a little shiver rippled over her at the still-potent memory of the heat in his eyes, the desperation in his hands, when he'd torn through her lingerie. No one had ever ripped away her bra, her panties, as if he couldn't wait another second to have her bare beneath him. He'd asked her—*told* her—what he wanted her to do, where to put her hands, even when to come for him...and it had been the greatest thrill of her life not only to do it all, but also to wait breathlessly for his next sensual command.

As she got out of her car, she took a deep breath of the salty-sweet sea air. It was time to make the shift from personal to professional, at least for a few hours. Coming back to his boathouse for their second interview was important not only so that she could ask him her follow-up questions, but also so that she could make sure she described the look and feel of his workspace properly.

Of course, that was right when she rounded the corner from the parking lot...and saw Dylan bent over sanding the side of the boat in the middle of his workshop, shirtless, his skin gleaming with sweat, his muscles rippling. Oh Lord.

Oh Lord.

She wanted his mouth, his hands, his body on hers again. Wanted to come apart for him, beneath him, against him, again and again.

Wanted to discover just how much more pleasure there was to be had in his arms.

She took another deep breath, and then one more for good measure. *Business.* She needed to stay on track with her story.

But, as she let the last slightly ragged breath go, she knew she was going to have to ride out a few more seconds of being a *very* attracted woman first.

Grace had read several books on boat building to make sure that she understood the basics, but watching Dylan painstakingly sand a section by hand, then run his other hand over the smooth wood before he moved on to the next plank, almost felt like watching a man with his lover. Every boat he made, she sensed, meant a great deal to him. Who was this one for? What man or woman would be lucky enough to sail away on a boat that had been so painstakingly created?

As a writer, Grace saw the world through words first. But as she watched him work, she could see what a fascinating documentary someone could make here with Dylan. Both the visual story of the creation of a boat from start to finish and an in-depth look into the mind of the man who could turn planks of wood into magic.

Of course, she could easily guess that he would never allow anyone to film him. Not because he was hiding anything. It was simply that for all that he'd opened his work and his family to her, Dylan was a naturally private man.

It was why sailing suited him so well. He didn't need accolades. Didn't need to be seen by anyone as the best. He simply wanted to be free to build boats. Free to race them. Free to sail off in one to explore whatever corner of the world interested him. And she didn't blame him for wanting to live his life according to his own rules when she wanted that very same thing—to live the life of her dreams without always looking in the shadows, without always worrying about being hurt.

"Good morning, Grace."

Dylan put the sandpaper down and turned to her with a smile. A very male smile that was just smug enough to tell her he knew she'd been there all along and had been happy to let her watch him work shirtless.

Both of them had been happy about it, she thought as she returned his smile. "Is now still a good time for our interview?"

"Sure, but where's Mason?"

"I booked a babysitter for him so that I could focus."

"I thought you were going to bring him. I've seen how my cousins set up safe areas so their kids can play at parties. I was planning on it."

He was sweet, so amazingly sweet to always think of including Mason. But even if her son could have played happily in a cordoned-off area of the boathouse while they did the interview, Grace had wanted to make sure that they couldn't just fall so easily into pretend-family time again. It would be too easy, she could already see, to slip into the fantasy that the three of them really were a unit.

This isn't forever, she reminded herself. One day Dylan would sail away while she and Mason stayed right here. But until then, they would appreciate every second with him.

"He seemed quite happy with the young, pretty babysitter, actually." Grace had repeatedly reminded herself in the past half hour that she couldn't watch over her son every single second. A couple of hours with a babysitter would be okay, even if leaving him this morning was one of the hardest things she'd ever done.

Grace moved farther into the boathouse. "Who is this boat for?"

"Promise you won't tell?"

She was the one frowning now. "If you don't want me to talk about something in my interview, of course I won't."

"No, that's not the reason." He reached out a hand and it felt so natural to take it. "It's for my family."

Surprised—and touched—she asked, "They don't know about it?"

"If they knew, they might think they needed to feel bad about me ignoring the waiting list for them."

"How long is your customer waiting list?"

He shrugged. "I'll take a look at it again next week."

"Why do I have the sense that you pay as much attention to your waiting list as you do to your ringing phone?"

"Because you already know me so well." He drew her closer. "I know you're here to interview me today, not to make out with me, but I've spent every second since Saturday night thinking about kissing you again. Just one and then we'll get down to business. I promise."

"Well," she said softly, "since you proved to me on Saturday night that you are good at keeping your promises, just one...since we really do need to get to the interview."

"Then I'll have to make it count, won't I?"

Before she could even take her next breath, his mouth was on hers. Arousing. Seducing. Ravaging. And challenging her to pour just as much passion back into him. Instinctively, she answered that challenge with so much heat and passion that before she knew it her arms were around his neck, her legs were wrapped around his waist, and his hands were on her hips to hold her steady against him while they tried to get as close to each other as they possibly could in the middle of his sun-drenched boathouse.

"Wow," she said slowly when he finally set her back on her feet and she tried to get her brain to fire on all cylinders again, "you really know how to make a kiss count, don't you?"

"I was going to say the same about you," he said in a hungry voice that sent another wave of desire shuddering through her.

"I think I'm going to need a minute for my head to clear." She shook her head and took a couple of deep breaths, but it didn't help clear the lust-filled fog from her brain. "Maybe two minutes."

"Would coffee help?"

"Hopefully, yes."

They both walked the short distance to his small corner kitchen, and while he brewed some seriously great-smelling coffee, she set up her recorder, pad of paper, and pen on the small table...and tried with all her might to stop thinking about how desperately she wanted to jump back into his arms.

He brought her a mug and she nearly groaned aloud with pleasure at how delicious it was. "Where did you learn to make coffee this good?"

"Good, strong coffee is the best way to wake crew members up for their watch."

For the next hour or so, she asked him much more practical nuts-and-bolts questions about sailing and boats than she'd asked him on Friday. Finally, she returned to something he'd said about continuing to teach new sailors the ropes. "I can see how much satisfaction there must be in building a boat, and I can imagine how exciting races must be. But why do you continue to teach when I'm guessing those hours would be better spent building a pricey sailboat for someone on your waiting list?"

"Early on, when I was trying to make a go of boat building, taking people out for a long weekend was an easy, fun way to bring in funding. I've always enjoyed sailing with a crew. Probably comes from having four siblings and more than a dozen cousins," he said with a grin. "The people who come out to learn with me are always an odd mix. Maybe one's a baker. Another's an accountant. A third is a painter. A fourth is a cop. They usually don't have much experience with sailing, but it doesn't matter because all of them—all of us—share the same passion. And by the time we make it back into the harbor, they're hooked."

"What do you tell them before you head out? What are your hard and fast rules for sailing?"

"There's just one: When it's your turn to stand watch, you show up on time. It's the only thing I'm an inflexible tyrant about because I've seen what happens when the watch system breaks down and people lose vital hours of sleep. Fatigue will kill you faster at sea than any storm will."

Grace was reminded yet again of the way Dylan had shifted on Saturday night from gentle to dominant, from sweet to dangerous. Obviously, he'd seen how much she liked it, but she also now knew that the sinfully sexy man who had ripped her panties off was just as much a part of him as the softhearted man who loved making her baby laugh. She could easily imagine him shifting from easygoing to no-bullshit in the blink of an eye if he thought anyone was putting his crew at risk out at sea. He was a natural-born protector.

"You really don't have any other rules?"

"I teach my clients navigation and heavy-weather sailing. How to plan a passage. But mostly, we just sail. That's how I learned best, not by listening to someone talk about technique, but by keeping the boat moving, one way or another. If the wind is from ahead, haul the sails in. If the wind is from the side or behind, let them out. It isn't much harder than that."

"You help make people's dreams a reality," she mused aloud. "That's why you do it, isn't it? Because you had that same dream once."

"I still do. I've never lost my sense of awe at what the ocean is capable of, not even after hundreds of midnight watches. As far as I'm concerned, the magic of a night sea is one that can only be matched, and transcended, by one thing." He paused and held her gaze for a long moment. "By love."

When heat—and emotion—immediately kicked up between them, Grace did what she could to bank it for the time being and hold her focus on her interview. Later, she knew, they would shift from professional to personal. But for now, she needed to be no-bullshit, too.

"I'm assuming your students have all come back in one piece?"

"The ocean has a way of rising up to test your resolve right when you think you've got everything dialed in. But even though there've been a couple of close calls here and there, I'm proud to say that my crews have not only come back in one piece, but many of them have also gone on to do some pretty major cruises in their own sailboats for months at a time."

"So then what do you teach them if not technique?"

"To stay flexible and to be willing to change tactics as conditions dictate, whether it's challenging weather or equipment failure. A good sailor knows that if the action you're taking isn't working, you try something else. And, most important, to enjoy the hell out of what you're doing, because every single moment is a gift."

Grace had thought interviewing Dylan would be a job, nothing more. But again and again he touched her heart with something he said, something he did. "Staying flexible and enjoying every moment are good rules not just for sailing, but for life," she agreed.

After all, wasn't that exactly what she'd done when she'd learned she was pregnant and would be raising her son on her own? She'd changed tactics and then made sure to enjoy the gift of every moment with Mason.

"My family taught me those rules," he told her.

"Out on a sailboat?"

He shook his head. "My father lost his job when I was pretty young. He was out of work for long enough that Ian ended up stepping up to keep things afloat. I was too young to be much help to anyone, but I watched. I learned. And I saw that the sacrifices everyone made for each other were more than worth it."

"The boat you're making for them is your way of saying thank you, isn't it?" But even as she said it, she knew it was more than that. "And it's also your way of sharing with them what has brought you endless joy."

"Yes," was his simple answer, one that made her heart feel even softer toward him—even more open with him. No other man had ever disarmed her so easily...or heated her up so quickly.

"Can you put it into words, that joy?"

"Everyone from Tennyson to Jacques Cousteau to Jimmy Buffett has said it already, better than I ever will."

"I'd like to hear it in your words, Dylan." Didn't he realize what a poet he was when he spoke about the sea? About his family? "Please."

He took her hands, stroked his fingers over them before he began to speak. "The sea is full of so much wonder and magic that I've never seen anyone leave one of my boats without falling under its spell. Even people who have been afraid before, or who are certain they will never find their sea legs. All I really want to do—all I really want to give to people—is that fearlessness, that respect, that love that I've always felt." He lifted her hands to his chest so that she could feel the strong, steady beat of his heart. "Right here."

The phone rang, jolting her out of the spell his words were weaving around her. But he made absolutely no move to answer it, didn't even seem to notice it.

"You're going to ignore that, aren't you? Doesn't it ever bother you, wondering who it is?"

"I've always found that the people I want to hear from know where to look for me. Just like you did."

The phone stopped ringing for a few seconds, then immediately started again. "You're not even going to check the caller ID?"

"What's caller ID?"

She knew he was kidding—he *must* be kidding, right? Fortunately, when the phone started ringing a third time, he said, "If you want to answer it, be my guest."

Of course she did, so she picked up the handset on the old phone, complete with spiral cord, that hung from the wall by the desk. "Hello."

"Hello, it's Shawna." The woman on the other end of the line managed to infuse a ridiculous amount of sexiness into the three words. "It would be *so* nice if you could let Dylan know I want to talk to him."

Grace figured out from less than a dozen words that this woman had been in Dylan's bed. And that knowledge made her feel so jealous *and* irritated that despite knowing Dylan hated speaking on the phone unless he absolutely had to, she said, "No problem, Shawna. Hold on and I'll pass him the phone."

She held out the receiver to him, trying to read whether or not he was pleased by the obvious booty call, but he had his poker face on. And it was a damned good one, too.

"Hi, Shawna." He listened to what she had to say before replying, "That's nice of you to think of me for the game tonight." Dylan paused and looked straight at Grace, his expression shifting from easy to intense in the blink of an eye. "But I'm seeing someone. Someone important. So I'm going to have to pass. Have fun at the game."

I'm seeing someone? she thought as he put down the phone. "You didn't have to turn down the tickets." *Someone important?* "You could have gone with her."

"Didn't you just hear me say that I'm taken?"

For all the warnings she'd given herself about taking things too seriously with Dylan, she couldn't stop a warm glow from washing over her. "I thought we agreed to take things slow."

"We are." He reached for her, drew her against him the way she'd been secretly longing for throughout their interview. "Slow and exclusive."

But as thrilled as she was to hear Dylan say that he wanted only her, she had to try to make sense of something that *didn't* make any sense. "How are you not with someone already?" She gestured to the phone. "Clearly, there are women lining up around the block for some time with you. And with the way you look, the way you kiss—" She made herself stop before she rambled on any longer about how amazing a catch he was. "I just don't understand it."

"I have all the same questions about you, Grace. The way you look. The way you kiss. The way I can't stop smiling whenever you're near. How are you still single?"

Was he nuts? The reason was obvious. "I'm a single mother of a ten-month-old." Not to mention the fact that she hadn't let anyone close enough to even try getting through the wall she'd put up around her heart after it had been smashed by her ex and his family.

"A great ten-month-old."

Dylan's affection for her son was yet another thing that set him a world apart from other men. "That's another thing I can't figure out."

"What's that?"

"How you are so willing to open up your life to a woman with baggage."

"Anyone who would actually call Mason *baggage*, anyone who can't see that he's the greatest gift in the world, doesn't deserve you." He brushed back a lock of her hair, making her shiver despite the heat. "Did you get what you needed for today's interview?"

With the way he was looking at her, she could only just manage to say, "Yes. We've covered a lot of ground today."

"Not enough." He took each of her hands in his and lifted them to his lips for a kiss before he started moving them both into the back area of the boathouse. "Not nearly enough."

CHAPTER FOURTEEN

"Is there—" My God, had anyone ever looked at her like this? Like he wanted to devour her in one big gulp and was only barely restraining himself from doing just that? "Is there something else you wanted to tell me?" But he didn't answer, simply continued their path behind the nearly finished sloop. Her heart was racing as she followed him. "Something you need to show—"

When he backed her up against the wall, then lifted her hands and arms above her head so that her back arched slightly and her breasts pressed into the hard wall of his chest, she swallowed the last word.

"This." He nipped at her lower lip, hard enough that it sent a blast of heat—and need— searing through her, head to toe. "I need to show you this." He nipped at her again, her chin this time, sending even more bright bolts of desire through her. "I need to show you how much I want you." He found her earlobe next with his teeth, and a low moan slipped from her lips. "How I haven't been able to stop thinking of you since Saturday night." He breathed her in once. Then once again. "Your scent...it drives me crazy." He scraped his stubble across her neck. "Your skin...it's so soft, so kissable."

That was when he finally brought his mouth back to hers and licked across the seam of her lips, making her half-gasp, half-moan at how good it felt.

"Again," he urged her as he lifted his mouth from hers only far enough to speak. "I need to hear it again."

The truth was that she was just as desperate for him, had barely been holding desire at bay long enough to get through her interview. Unable to take any more teasing, she took the next kiss he gave her deeper. So deep, so fast, that she was surprised a spark didn't actually light between them to set his boathouse on fire.

She knew better than to do this, to let him reach for the hem of the sundress she was wearing and pull it up over her head in the middle of the day, at his place of business, where someone could walk in at any moment. But once again, her need for him was bigger than her fears. So big that she found herself relishing this chance for a few wicked moments, for one more break from the straight and narrow line she'd been walking for the past year and a half.

The truth was that knowing someone might walk into his boathouse, might come looking for him and find them wrapped all around each other, only made it more exciting. And as she embraced the wildness of the moment, she realized it didn't just feel okay to stop being so careful all the time—it felt like exactly what she needed.

Especially when he ran his big hands over her curves and told her how perfect, how pretty she was, that he couldn't get enough of her, that she was all he could think about. Every word, every touch, made her lose her breath a little more as he rained kisses on her skin between each sweet murmur. His lips feathered across her cheek, her neck, her collarbone, and then the swell of her breasts before he clicked open the latch on her bra and cupped her breasts together so that he could lave both needy peaks at once.

One kiss, one taste had quickly spiraled into a desperate need for more. So much more. Which meant that when he slowly lowered himself to his knees before her, his hands gripping her hips hard as he held her right where he wanted her against the wall, his lips running a devastating path over her ribs and stomach, she didn't stop him. Couldn't, frankly, have imagined a world in which the word *stop* could possibly have come out of her mouth.

Especially when he leaned in and pressed his lips to the vee between her legs, lace and all.

"Oh...oh...oh..."

It didn't matter how many times he loved her like that. Every time would feel like the first. Explosive and shockingly sinful from the first touch of his tongue to her overheated flesh. And when he moved away just enough to slide the damp lace down her thighs, the anticipation of knowing his tongue was going to slick across her bare skin soon nearly did her in.

He found her with his fingers at the exact moment he used his lips and tongue to take her higher, and then higher still. She'd never done anything this exciting, this thrilling. Only in her secret sexy fantasies had she believed anything like this could happen. And yet here she was, on the verge of climaxing with Dylan kneeling between her legs while she stood in front of him wearing only heels, the sunlight from his skylights beaming down on the top of his head as he took her places she hadn't even realized she could go.

"Now," he urged as he continued to play over her so perfectly with his fingers. "Come for me now, Grace."

As if her body had only been waiting for his sensual command, she held on to his shoulders for dear life as he made her shake and gasp and come apart at the very seams. Wave after wave of pleasure rocked over her, through her, until her legs couldn't support her anymore and it was only Dylan's hold on her that kept her up against the wall.

She was only vaguely aware that he was kissing his way back up her body, his hands steady on her hips the whole time so that she didn't have to count on her shaky legs to hold her up. His kisses were soft and lingering as he let her catch her breath, but she wasn't so far gone that she could miss the need throbbing through him. Yet again, he was restraining himself from taking what *he* needed.

"You must have been so frustrated on Saturday night, after the way you left without me returning the favor."

"Touching you, feeling you, watching you come apart is the most fulfilled I've ever been in my life. Anything more is just a bonus."

"In that case," she said in a husky voice, "it looks like it's time for a bonus. Not just for you, but for me. Because you weren't the only one who was frustrated. I wanted to take your clothes off. I wanted to touch you." She paused, held his gaze. "I wanted to make you come."

She could feel his heartbeat kick up even faster against her hand as he said, "I want you, Grace. You know how much I want you, how much I want all of those things, too. But I don't want to make the mistake of pushing you too far, too fast. You weren't ready for more Saturday night."

"You're right, I wasn't ready then. But now, I am."

She didn't want to be the only one seduced. She wanted to seduce, too. So that they were equals. So that she would stop feeling so off-balance. And so she would finally know whether he tasted as good as she'd fantasized he would.

"I need more. I need you the way you've had me."

Her eyes on his, she lifted his hands from her hips so that she could lower herself to her knees on the wood-planked floor.

* * *

Dylan lived only a couple of blocks from his boathouse. But he hadn't been able to wait long enough to travel those two blocks with Grace, to take those five minutes before stripping off her clothes. Instead, he'd given in—yet again—to his inner caveman and dragged her to the back of his workshop to strip her clothes away.

She'd said she needed to take things slow, but every time fierce desire drove them into another heated kiss, he felt her revel in the thrill of being with him. He loved watching her embrace her innate sensuality, the very same sensual woman she'd believed was forever dead because some asshole she used to date had a heart and soul made out of coal.

But even after she'd let herself go in the most beautiful way he'd ever seen, with her dress and lingerie lying on the wood-planked floor where he'd dropped them, he hadn't expected this. Hadn't thought she'd slide down the wall, naked but for her heels and flushed from her climax, to go on her knees in front of him.

Her hands were totally steady, and determined, as she worked on his belt buckle. He'd been on the edge for so long, since the moment he'd first set eyes on her outside his boathouse, that he wouldn't need much more to go off than this brush of her fingers over his denim-covered erection while he looked down at her beautiful naked body.

Her eyes were glittering with excitement and arousal as she smiled up at him. Just the thought of her pulling him free and wrapping her lips around him...

He had to close his eyes for a few seconds to try to get a grip, but even then he couldn't stop his hands from threading through her soft hair as she worked his zipper open. The sound she made as she wrapped her fingers around him, a hum of deep pleasure that resonated all the way through his entire body, nearly sent him over.

He couldn't speak, couldn't move, couldn't do anything but stare down at Grace in awe. But she read his mind, thank God, understood that he wasn't going to last long this time. And when she leaned forward another couple of inches and took him into her mouth?

Jesus.

Nothing had ever felt this good. Not one damned thing in thirty-one years could compete with her soft lips, her wet tongue, the heat and pull of her mouth as she loved him the same way he'd just loved her.

His hands tightened in her hair as hers tightened on his hips. Time ceased to move forward. He wasn't even sure he was breathing anymore, as everything came down to this moment. This pleasure. This woman.

Grace. Grace. Grace.

Everything inside of him exploded, blindingly bright and colorful. He'd never experienced a storm so wild, or one so precious.

Moments later he was on his knees with her, their kisses even more passionate for all they'd just given—and taken—from each other. Only when the sound of footsteps came and he heard someone say his name was he able to drag his mouth from hers.

He looked into her eyes, still beautifully hazy with pleasure. "Someone's here." He knew they needed to get their clothes back on, but he couldn't stop himself from giving her another kiss before, and after, each word.

The second time the visitor called his name, her eyes went wide as what he'd just said finally registered. "Someone's here," she echoed.

Grace scrambled for her dress, but Dylan was already drawing it over her head. They were both on their feet again, her lingerie shoved into the pocket of his jeans, when his visitor poked his head around the hull of the boat and saw them in the back corner.

"Ah, there you are, Dylan. Grace, it's good to see you again."

His brother Adam looked far too pleased by what he saw. Dylan had walked in on his brother once when they were teens, and he had no doubt his brother saw this as payback.

Grace's skin was flushed, both from their kisses and from obvious embarrassment at nearly being caught without their clothes on, but Dylan was impressed by the lift of her chin. Her strength had drawn him from the start, and he loved the way she calmly met his brother's eyes.

"It's good to see you, too, Adam," she said smoothly, despite the fact that her underwear was stuffed into Dylan's jeans pocket.

"I hope I'm not interrupting anything," his brother said, even though he knew damn well that he was.

Grace raised an eyebrow in Adam's direction, the same look he'd seen her give Mason once when he was misbehaving at the aquarium. A warning not to mess with her. "Actually," she said with a small smile, "your timing was perfect." Turning back to Dylan, she said, "I need to get back to my babysitter now."

He wanted to reach for her, wanted his brother—and the rest of the world—to know for sure that she wasn't just a journalist doing a story on him or just a sexy fling. She was *his.* And yet, he knew he couldn't force anything, knew that no matter the physical barriers they'd begun to knock down between them, she'd only resent him if he tried to push her faster than she was ready to go.

Thankfully, though, instead of simply walking away, she reached up to put her hand on his face and then went on her tippy-toes in her heels to press her mouth to his in a soft kiss. She was smiling when she pulled back. "'Bye."

* * *

"I knew when you called us together last night that things were serious," Adam said, "but seeing you two together today? Love at first sight has clearly struck again. It's like an epidemic in this family."

Dylan only grinned. "You know what they say—the longer you hold out, the harder you fall. Which means you're going to be dust when it happens to you."

"Nope," Adam insisted. "At least one of us has to keep having fun. Do you know what you're doing, gunning for a ready-made family with Grace and Mason?"

Adam might think he was happy with his parade of one-night stands who had nothing of substance to say outside of the bedroom, but his brother didn't have a damn clue what he was missing. No-strings fun got real old, real fast.

Grace's beauty, her innate sensuality, had been what had drawn Dylan in at first. And every time they touched, he knew how perfectly matched they were as man and woman. But it was her resilience and strength that had solidified his knowledge that she was the right woman to go the distance with. He'd grown up with a strong woman leading their family, and he couldn't imagine settling for anything less than the example their mother had provided. Grace was everything he could ever have wanted. Everything he could ever have wished for.

"If there was a chance that she'd agree to marry me today, I'd jump at it."

Adam studied him for a moment before nodding. "She makes you happy. A different kind of happy than you've always been."

"Trust me, you'll understand once it happens to you."

Deliberately ignoring that last statement, Adam said, "While nearly walking in on the two of you going at it was fun, I'm here because I've got a favor to ask. Turns out the city is planning to tear down the old Maritime Museum to rebuild something flashy and modern."

Dylan frowned. "I thought that had been tabled for the time being so that more people could weigh in."

"Not according to what I just heard this morning from a friend on the board."

"The place needs a hell of a lot of work, but there's major history in that building."

"I know. That's why I'm going to convince them to let me restore it instead. Which is where you come in. You not only speak their language, but you've built boats for half the people on the board. They're having a cocktail event in a couple of days. It would be great if you and Grace could come."

"I'm in, and I'll check with Grace," Dylan said. "In return, I could use an extra pair of hands putting the final coat of urethane on the boat."

"Man, this sloop is a beauty," Adam said, already rolling up his sleeves to help. "You've built some great boats, but I think this one might be your finest yet. Your client is one lucky S.O.B."

Dylan grinned, said, "I agree," and for the next few hours enjoyed working side by side with his brother on a boat that he had no idea was already his.

CHAPTER FIFTEEN

Grace wrote like crazy the next day while Mason napped. She hadn't yet finished transcribing yesterday's interview with Dylan, but she wanted to make some forward progress, so she started writing. The saying went that it was easier to edit a page with words on it, rather than a blank one, and doing the bulk of her writing while Mason slept meant she'd gotten used to creativity on command. Unfortunately, ninety minutes later, as she reread what she'd written so far, she wasn't particularly impressed with any of it.

Maybe she simply needed to get up from her computer for a little while. She went into the kitchen to pour herself another cup of coffee, but as she brought it to her lips she realized she didn't want it. It was the same with the trusty Hershey's Kisses she kept in the freezer. A little chocolate melting on her tongue wouldn't do anything to cure her restlessness, or a mind that was jumping around.

It wasn't creativity on command that was messing with her productivity. Nor was the problem the fairly tight deadline for the cover story. It was the fact that her head—and body— were still reeling from being with Dylan yesterday. From the risks they'd taken...and how much she'd loved every second of taking those risks, even if she shouldn't have, and they'd nearly been caught naked in each other's arms by his brother.

She'd been spinning from Dylan's taste, from everything he'd said both during the interview and then after, when her clothes were coming off and his were, too. Now, she forced herself to admit the real reason she hadn't wanted to transcribe the interview today: She'd been afraid of what hearing his voice would do to her. Of what it would make her feel.

Because she was already feeling so much. *Too much.*

Grace had never fallen so fast for anyone. Never thought it was possible to begin to care so deeply for someone so quickly—or to crave him so wholly—especially when she, of all people, should know better than to lose her head, or her heart, over another handsome, charismatic man.

Only, even as she thought it, she knew she wasn't being fair to Dylan. Yes, he was handsome. Yes, he was powerful. But he was so much more than just that. He was fun. He was sweet. He was talented. He was devoted to his family. He was adorable with Mason. And he wanted to protect them both.

Yesterday in his boathouse, when she'd taken him the same way he'd taken her, she'd hoped that giving him pleasure would help her feel more in control. Less off-balance. But it hadn't worked. Not in the slightest, given that she'd left his boathouse as far off-balance as she'd ever been.

Mostly because she couldn't stop rethinking everything—everything she'd been so sure about since Mason. Namely that she had to be strong all by herself. And that she had to pay for her stupidity with her ex by always doing the safe thing, by remaining in perfect control forevermore.

Knowing Mason would be up soon, and that her deadline wasn't going anywhere regardless of how twisted up she felt inside, she was sitting back down behind her computer when she knocked her notebook to the floor. Reaching for it, she realized it had fallen open to a William Shakespeare quote from *Much Ado About Nothing*.

> *Sigh no more, ladies, sigh no more,*
> *Men are deceivers ever,*
> *One foot in sea and one on shore,*
> *To one thing constant never.*

Dylan, she already knew, would never willingly deceive her, would never reel her in just for a laugh. But at his core he was a sailor. One whom she doubted would ever be as happy on land as he was out on the sea. Sailing was considered to be the great escape. And after all, wasn't that when Dylan had turned to sailing— when his father had lost his job, times had been rough for his family, and it had become his passion, as well?

And yet, at the same time, how could she forget what he'd said yesterday during their second interview: *"The magic of a night sea is one that can only be matched, and transcended, by one thing. By love."*

As if Mason knew that his mother was desperate for a distraction from thoughts that were careening from one end of her mind to the other, he woke up from his nap. After a quick diaper change, she gathered up a snack, a bottle, and a change of clothes and put them all in the bottom of his stroller.

"What do you say you and I head out to the park and let some fresh air clear our heads?"

Her son's eyes lit up at the word *park* just as her phone rang. When she saw Dylan's name on the screen, she knew she lit up in exactly the same way.

She should probably let it ring, give herself a little space to keep thinking things through. But from the first, Dylan had been a gift she hadn't been able to deny herself. Or her son, whom she'd seen laugh more with him than with anyone else.

"I was sitting here missing you and Mason," Dylan told her when she picked up, "so I thought I'd call." Mason giggled as she handed him his stuffed giraffe and accidentally knocked him in the nose with its fluffy tail. "Your kid has the best laugh."

"He really does, doesn't he?"

"He gets it from his beautiful mother."

It felt as though Dylan knew every secret code to unlock all the locked-down parts of her heart. And even when she knew she should make sure the two of them stuck to *slow,* it was the last thing she wanted—and not just because every kiss, every caress he gave her felt so good. Just being with Dylan made her happy.

Happier than she'd been in a very long time.

"We're going to the playground if you want to take a little break."

"The playground sounds like the perfect place to celebrate."

"Celebrate?" She quickly guessed, "Are you done with the boat?"

"Adam helped me with a few finishing touches last night."

"He's going to be so thrilled when he finds out it's his. When are you going to tell them all?"

"Soon. Once I return from my trip to Australia, everyone else should be back in Seattle again, too."

"You're going to *Australia?*" She realized, too late, that she sounded like a girlfriend trying to keep track of her boyfriend's schedule.

"I leave Thursday for a seven-hundred-mile yacht race out of Sydney. I'll only be gone a week, but I'm going to miss you and Mason like crazy, Grace. If I hadn't promised my friend a year ago that I'd do this—"

"The race sounds amazing," she said, ruthlessly pushing away the ache inside of her at the thought of not seeing Dylan for an entire week. *Fun,* she reminded herself. They were just having fun, enjoying each other while they were working together on her magazine article.

And that was all she could let herself believe it was for now, because fun wasn't something she needed to overthink. Fun wasn't something she needed to worry over. Fun wasn't something she needed to have a foolproof plan or an escape hatch nailed down for.

"I'll have a little over a week left to finish my story after you return, so hopefully you'll come back with some good stories for me."

Just then, Mason threw his giraffe and she knew he was tired of being strapped into his stroller without going anywhere. "We'll be at the playground right across the street. See you soon."

And despite not yet knowing exactly how to get a handle on her relationship with Dylan— one that already felt so much more important than any *fun* fling she'd ever had—it was a thrill to know that she would.

* * *

Fifteen minutes later, Mason was happily tucked into a toddler swing and squealing with joy as she pushed him higher and higher. He was a little daredevil, much like her parents had always said she'd been as a child, and she vowed never to let her own fears hold him back. She would support him in everything, no matter how dangerous or wild. Just as she had learned that Claudia Sullivan had done with her children.

The urge to protect her son from anything that might hurt him was all-consuming. But she knew better, knew that if her parents had still been alive, they'd have urged her to remember that giving him wings to fly was just as important as keeping him safe.

Or, she thought with a little smile, maybe he'd end up choosing a boat in which to sail across the deep blue sea. Lost in her thoughts, it wasn't until Mason started making happy little sounds that she realized Dylan was walking straight toward them. She heard a collective gasp of female appreciation from the other women in the park as he stepped onto the sandy playground in jeans and a T-shirt that fit him so well her own mouth went dry. Not in the least because she finally knew *exactly* how good he looked *without* said jeans and T-shirt.

He grabbed Mason's swing in midair, and her son puckered up for a kiss. That kiss was always the first thing Mason wanted, and it never failed to move her how easily and sweetly affectionate Dylan was with her little boy.

When Mason looked over his shoulder at her, Dylan grinned and said, "One for him, one for you."

Setting Mason back to flying in his swing with one hand, he used the other to pull her close, then kissed her slowly and deeply in front of everyone...sending her heart flying, too.

CHAPTER SIXTEEN

When they were finally able to take Mason away from the park without too much of a fuss, the three of them headed to the ice cream shop. Playing at the park. Getting ice cream. Sharing hot kisses. *See*, Grace told herself, *we're just having fun.*

Leaving Mason sitting proudly like a big boy beside Dylan outside the ice cream store with his little legs sticking straight out in front of him on the brightly painted bench, she went inside and placed their orders. Five minutes later, she returned with her hands full.

"Here's your rainbow sorbet, sweet pea." Mason reached for the cone and immediately shoved it against his lips, bright green, orange, and pink streaks smearing his chubby cheeks. "And our banana split and two lemonades."

She usually just got a vanilla cone because the split was way too much for one person. But when Dylan had suggested they share the split, it hit her that she wasn't alone anymore. At least not for as long as whatever they were doing together lasted. Certainly as long as it took her to write the magazine story, she figured. And after? Well...she'd learned a year and a half ago that no matter how much you wanted to predict the future, there were some things you simply couldn't plan for.

Fun, she reminded herself yet again. That's all this was. All it needed to be.

Seeing that Dylan had Mason's sticky face well in hand with the container of wet wipes he'd found at the bottom of the stroller, she sat on his other side. When he'd finished cleaning Mason up, she lifted her lemonade.

"Congratulations on your newest creation." He clinked his cup against hers, and then she leaned over to kiss him softly, as natural a move as it had been to walk down the street from the park to the ice cream shop with her baby playing happily in his stroller in front of them.

"Speaking of creations, how's your article going?"

"Good."

He raised an eyebrow. "That was the least good-sounding *good* I've ever heard."

She dug her spoon into the strawberry scoop at the end of the dish and amended her reply to, "I did so much research before I began to interview you and you've given me so much great stuff...it should be coming together much more quickly than it is."

"We've got to get you out in one of my boats. I promise you, that will change everything."

Her heart skittered at the suggestion, because that was exactly what she was afraid would happen if she sailed with Dylan. That *everything would change.* That she'd lose hold of her "just having fun" perspective. That she'd start to want more than pleasure and laughter. And that she'd only be setting up herself and Mason for a huge fall.

"I'll be back from Australia on the Saturday after next, so why don't we schedule our sail for the following Sunday? That way you'll still have nearly a week to polish up your story if you need to."

Nearly two weeks was enough time to mentally prepare herself for their sail. It had to be. "Okay, I'll book a babysitter."

"You do realize that my mother was serious when she offered to watch Mason anytime you needed her to, don't you?"

"Claudia is very sweet and generous, and Mason obviously loved playing with her, but—"

"It will make her day knowing she'll get to see him again."

When he put it that way, how could she keep arguing? "My mother would have felt the same way." It was a beautiful sunny day, and she was eating ice cream with her perfect son and the gorgeous man she was having "fun" with. She shouldn't feel sad. Still, she'd never figured out how to shake her sorrow that both her parents were gone.

Obviously, Dylan sensed it, because he put his hand over hers and said, "They see him, Grace. And you, too, the daughter they've always been so proud of. Watching you raise Mason...I know they're prouder of you than ever."

The sun, the ice cream, the smile on her son's face, Dylan's hand over hers—all helped her hold the tears at bay. "I had a friend in high school who came from a big family, and she hated it. Hated the lack of privacy. Hated that someone was always into her things. My parents tried for more kids, but my mother couldn't..." No, she absolutely refused to ruin their afternoon by breaking down. She focused instead on slicing off a piece of banana from the split and feeding it to Mason between his own licks of sorbet. "What I'm trying to say is that you're very lucky to have such a close family."

"I agree," he said. "Although I'm a little pissed off at my brother Adam right now."

"Why? I thought he helped you with the boat yesterday."

"He did, but only after he walked in on us, which meant you put your clothes on long before I was ready." She was blushing by the time he added, "And I was planning to ask you on our first official date for tomorrow night, but it turns out that Adam needs the two of us to go with him to a swanky cocktail party at the old Maritime Museum, put on by the board members. They're thinking of tearing it down and putting up a modern glass and steel showcase. He wants us to help talk them out of that and into letting him get his hands on it to restore the building."

"I'm glad he wants to fight to save the historic building. It's a truly beautiful one. And it makes perfect sense that he'd want you there. But why would he want me to come?"

"You're smart. You're beautiful. And I'm guessing that, from the way you research the topics that you write about, you already know more about the history of Seattle sailing than anyone on the museum's board." He leaned forward to lick a drop of ice cream from her lips. "Come with me tomorrow night, Grace. We'll do the rounds for my brother as fast as we can, then sneak off and have our own private night on the town without anyone from my family around this time."

The brush of his tongue against her sensitive skin had knocked her brain cells off-balance, far enough that she couldn't quite focus on what her answer to his question should be.

"Say yes," he murmured against her lips as he leaned in again to kiss her this time.

Spinning even faster now, she said, "You're doing this on purpose. Making it hard for me to think."

He nuzzled her earlobe. "Is it working?"

"Almost."

But what he was asking her was too important to be decided on a dizzy, aroused whim.

A date.

She hadn't been on one of those in a really long time. Dinner at his parents' house had been an interview, though it had ended with a kiss. And the aquarium hadn't started as a date, either, though it had ended with much more than just one kiss. Even this trip to the ice cream store could simply have been two friends and a baby out for an afternoon break. A *fun* break for sun and sugar in the middle of the day. Friends with benefits, but still nothing official. Not a date that could potentially lead to so much more.

"Tell me I'm going too fast, Grace, and I swear I'll figure out a way to back off and give you more space."

It should have been exactly the right thing for him to say. But she was shocked to realize that the thought of Dylan backing off had her gut clenching far tighter than did the risk of dating him.

Was she wary about going down that road with anyone again? Yes, and she'd be crazy not to be. But she had to start to live again at some point, didn't she? And having a full life didn't only mean stolen kisses and crazy hot orgasms.

"Yes," she said, smiling up at the man who had been waiting none too patiently for her answer. "I'd love to go on a date with you tomorrow night."

Dylan sealed her affirmative reply with a kiss that was hot enough to melt what was left of their ice cream. At least until Mason climbed between them, planting wet, sticky kisses on both of their cheeks.

* * *

Grace was still smiling ten minutes later as she headed for their apartment with Mason falling asleep in his stroller. Before they'd parted, Dylan had quickly pulled out his cell phone and checked in with his mother about babysitting both tomorrow night and then again during their sail when Dylan returned from Australia in a couple of weeks. If Grace'd had any doubt that Claudia would be excited to see Mason again, his mother's happy exclamations—loud enough for Grace to hear from the other side of the bench—put them to rest.

After Dylan had left to meet with a potential new client, she'd been walking around with a silly smile on her face. At least until she realized that she had absolutely *nothing* to wear!

Grace had a few nice dresses from before she'd gotten pregnant, but even on the off chance that they still fit her new post-baby curves, all of them had been dresses she'd worn for Richard. Deciding to box them up to give away when she got back to their apartment, she accepted that she was going to have to make a dent in her savings with a new outfit. She'd put every spare penny into her just-in-case legal defense fund for the past year and a half. With the money coming in from the cover story, she could let herself spend a teeny bit on this special night with Dylan, couldn't she?

Fashion was yet another thing she hadn't given much thought to since having Mason. Grace looked down at her jeans and striped blue and white top and knew that she managed to look pretty or professional when she needed to. But she hadn't gone for *sexy* in a very long time.

Making a slight detour from her apartment building toward the nearby shopping street, she reminded herself that while sexy would certainly be exciting, she really shouldn't break the bank, because simple and pretty would be good enough, right? Of course, that was right when she caught sight of a beautifully dressed boutique window, one that had the most incredible dress on display. The color was what struck her first—not red, not pink, but the best of both hues. The straps were braided lace and silk, a delicate pattern that continued through the bodice. A slim, shiny belt the same color as the fabric wound around the waist, further emphasizing the floaty skirt of the dress, which ended just below the knee.

It probably cost a fortune, but in spite of that, she still couldn't stop herself from pushing Mason's stroller inside the store.

"Welcome to Indulgence."

It was, Grace thought, the perfect name for a store in which every single item on display made her yearn.

The woman's face lit up as she looked down at Mason strapped into his stroller, clutching his stuffed giraffe in his sticky little fist. His head was turned to the side in sleep, his eyes closed so that his lashes looked a mile long.

"Your son is absolutely gorgeous," the woman whispered, clearly in an effort not to wake him up. "If you're thinking about trying on the dress in the window, I already know you're going to look *amazing* in it. And I swear I'm not just saying that because this is my store."

Grace knew what looked good on her. This dress would make Dylan's eyes pop out of his head. That alone would be worth the dent it made in her savings.

The store owner, who introduced herself as Colbie, correctly guessed Grace's size, and a very short while later was oohing and ahhing over how great she looked in the dress. "One more thing," Colbie said, leaving the dressing room for a few moments and returning with what had to be the greatest pair of shoes ever made. The leather on the high-heeled sandals was a super-soft gold and braided in a pattern very similar to the bodice and straps of the dress. "You're a size eight shoe, aren't you?"

Grace was already reaching for the sexy sandals as she nodded. She felt like a princess straight out of a fairy tale in this dress, these shoes. She'd just close her eyes when she signed the credit card slip and wouldn't let herself think about the bill until it came at the end of the month. She'd make it up by working doubly hard on the story about Dylan, doing such a great job with it that, hopefully, she'd turn this cover story into the first of many.

"I'll take them both."

Besides, even though being able to put money away for Mason was hugely important, wasn't feeling like a sexy woman again—and proving to herself that her ex hadn't stolen that from her—also something she should have prioritized long before now?

Which was why, when a luxurious lingerie set also caught her eye on her way to the register, she added it to her pile of goodies. Because really, what good were the gorgeous dress and perfect shoes if what Dylan found when he stripped her out of them at the end of their date wasn't just as pretty?

Her entire body flamed at the thought, already revving with anticipation of her date with Dylan. A date that suddenly felt as though it couldn't come soon enough.

CHAPTER SEVENTEEN

Dylan's mind had been blown by Grace from the start, but when she opened the door for him the following night, he swore his remaining brain cells actually melted inside his skull. If he could have thought clearly, he might have been able to stop his hands from grabbing, his mouth from devouring. But he didn't have a prayer of doing anything but kissing her until he'd managed to have at least a tiny part of his fill.

"I'm torn, Grace. So damned torn between staying right here to strip that beautiful dress off you and taking you out to show you off."

The way she smiled up at him only made it harder to think straight. "You look really good in your suit, too."

Mason crawled over then, grabbing fistfuls of Dylan's dark slacks to pull himself up. "I didn't forget about you, buddy," Dylan said as he lifted Mason into his arms. "I'm just having a hard time dealing with how stunning your mommy is." When Mason babbled something unintelligible, Dylan nodded. "You're right, I don't stand a chance of ever getting used to how beautiful she is, so I should stop trying." He kissed Mason on the forehead. "And since my mom will never forgive me if we don't bring you over, especially since she bought out the entire toy store downtown to spoil you rotten tonight, I guess that means we should head out."

He grabbed Mason's baby bag in his free hand and worked to get a grip on himself while Grace picked up her small gold purse from the entry table. She was halfway to the Jeep when she looked over her shoulder and said, "You should know that I was just as torn when I saw you standing on my front step."

Just like that, any control he'd managed to regain shattered.

* * *

Adam's date for the evening—a brunette that Dylan hadn't seen before tonight—looked anything but pleased by the way his brother's jaw dropped when the two of them walked in. Grace's beauty was only more stunning because she didn't seem to be aware that she turned heads everywhere she went. No wonder that prick who'd gotten her pregnant had wanted her. Rage wasn't something that came easily to Dylan, but ever since she'd told him what her ex and his family had done, fury kept rising up in him again and again.

Grace turned to look at him with concern on her beautiful face. "Is everything okay?"

"Not just okay," he told her as he cupped the nape of her neck and drew her mouth to his. "Perfect."

Kissing her here, with everyone's eyes on them, was a blatant signal to all the other men in the room. *She's mine,* was what he was telling them all. *All mine.*

He loved that one kiss was all it took for her eyes to go hazy with desire. So much desire that she whispered, "How long do we have to stay?"

He brought her mouth to his again before saying, "Thirty minutes. Forty-five tops. We'll do the rounds, make Adam's restoration pitch, and then we'll—"

His brother and his date interrupted them just then. After Adam made the introductions, he told Grace, "I hope you're planning to stick around, because I'm not sure I'll be able to scrape my brother off the floor if you don't." He didn't give Grace time to adjust to the weight of his comment, just asked her what he could get her to drink from the bar.

"A glass of white wine would be lovely."

"Your dress is gorgeous." Adam's date hadn't been able to take her eyes off Grace, either. "So are your shoes. I've got to know, where did you pick them up?"

Grace smiled at the woman. Dylan didn't get the sense that she noticed the other woman's envy at all—probably because she didn't see herself as someone of whom another woman would be jealous.

"A fabulous store downtown called Indulgence."

The name pricked through Dylan's brain. "Mia's best friend owns that store. Colbie Michaels. Actually, Colbie Bryant now that she's married our friend Noah."

"Wow, that's amazing," Grace said, smiling even wider now. "She was so nice. And I could have easily bankrupted myself in her store."

"Mia said her stock was great, and I can see she wasn't kidding." He'd also heard from both Mia and his brother Rafe that Indulgence sold some seriously sexy stuff beyond dresses and shoes. Had Grace bought anything else?

Dylan couldn't wait to find out, after he finally had a chance to strip her out of her pretty new dress.

By then, Adam's date had pulled out her phone and looked up the store's website. "Oh my God, Indulgence is having an evening sidewalk sale. Tonight only!"

Dylan could barely hold back his grin as his brother returned with their drinks, a glass of wine for Grace and beers for each of them. He'd been thinking a little karmic payback was in order for the way his brother had been so pleased to walk in on them in the boathouse a couple of days ago.

Adam turned to his date with his most charming smile to hand her a glass of champagne, but she was already saying, "I'm afraid I won't be able to stay."

He frowned, still holding out the glass of champagne for her. "Why not?"

She looked a little guilty for a moment before she shrugged. "You're a great guy, but I think we can both already tell that we just don't have the kind of spark that would last beyond a night or two. Not like Dylan and Grace," she said with a nod toward the two of them. "Anyone can see that they're the real deal. You and me, we'd just be a fling. I'm sure you'd be a great one-night stand, but I'm thinking it's time to start holding out for Mr. Right instead. I'll see myself out."

She was gone so fast she nearly gave his brother whiplash. "What the hell happened while I was getting everyone drinks?" Adam asked them.

Dylan finally lost the battle with his laughter. "Trust me, you don't want to know. It will only make you feel like less of a man than you already do. So, who do you need Grace and me to talk to?"

He had to admire the way his brother pulled it together so fast. Adam had always been good at compartmentalizing. Work rarely bubbled over into the rest of his life. And emotions never tangled with sex. Although, Dylan figured it was a big part of the reason why his brother's date had decided a dress sale would be a better way to spend the night.

Making the rounds ended up taking more than forty-five minutes, but Dylan greatly enjoyed listening to Grace talk about the history of the Maritime Museum and the important part the building had played in shaping the Seattle waterfront. He could see light bulbs going on over the heads of the board members as she spoke so eloquently about the history all around them. No one had ever made Adam's job of pitching for an historic renovation so easy.

"You're amazing," Adam said as he led them over to a gray-haired couple standing by the corner window.

"Once Dylan told me what you were trying to do, I have to admit I studied up a little."

"A little?" His brother was full of admiration. "You could write a book on the place."

Dylan thought he saw a light bulb go on over *her* head then. "You're right—there are so many interesting stories about this building and the men and women who have come through here over the years. Romantic ones, too, like Mr. and Mrs. Callam meeting and falling in love here."

"When I get the project," Adam said, "I'm going to push for you to do a companion book."

"That sounds amazing," she said, but he could see that the lingering connection with his brother worried her, too. Because for all that she might want to believe in honesty, in romance and lasting love, her brush with the Bentley family had taught her just the opposite.

It was up to Dylan and his family to give her back her faith in truth and love again. Fortunately, if anyone could do it, the Sullivans could.

Dylan's cell phone rang with Rafe's ring tone, a call he'd been waiting for.

"Is it your mother?" Grace immediately asked.

Knowing what a big deal it was for her to leave Mason with anyone, he gently stroked her cheek. "It's Rafe. And even though I'm sure Mason's doing great with my mom, why don't you give them a call while I talk to my brother?"

"And here I didn't think I was being nearly that obvious."

"There's nothing wrong with wanting to know your kid is safe. My mom used to check in on us a half-dozen times when they'd go out. Granted," he said with a grin, "that might have been because we had a history of doing things like jumping off the roof and starting huge bonfires in the backyard."

Her easy laughter warmed him as they both drew out their cell phones and headed to the deck that faced the water. While she called his mother to check in, he dialed Rafe. Unfortunately, everything his brother told him over the next several minutes made the fury that he'd barely shoved down earlier rise up again. Hotter than ever.

Grace's smile was a mile wide when she turned to him after they'd both hung up just seconds apart. "Look at the cute picture your mom took of Mason playing the piano. Doesn't he look like such a big boy? And so proud of himself for making music all by himself."

Looking at Mason's innocent face only made Dylan's gut twist tighter. "Rafe just confirmed for me that you weren't the only one, Grace."

She looked up from her phone. "I wasn't the only one what?" But before he could explain, understanding dawned. "Rafe has checked into my ex and his family, hasn't he?" Pain flashed across her face, clearly illuminated by the nearly full moon above them.

"Rafe found just what we thought he would." Dylan hadn't been able to keep his hands off her all night, but now, when he drew her against him, even while the attraction was still pulsing, this embrace was simply to reassure both of them. "More women. Many women."

"Did he...does he have any other children?" He could see one thought moving quickly to the next. "Does Mason have any half brothers or half sisters?"

"No. At least from everything Rafe picked through, it looks like none of the other women were as strong as you. They all took the money and did what the family wanted them to do."

He could see her heart breaking for all those other women in pure empathy. "They were probably too scared not to."

It was amazing that she didn't see the other women as weak. He also knew that she was right—pressure that strong from such a powerful family would break nearly anyone. But not her. Not his Grace.

"Why didn't I see it? Why didn't I see through him? Through the fancy dates where he never let me meet anyone? Not his friends. Definitely not his family."

"For as much as I despise the guy," Dylan said softly, "the truth is that I'm glad you trusted him. For long enough, at least, to create Mason."

"Richard and his parents have no idea about all the joy, all the wonder that they tried to destroy because my bloodline wasn't pure enough for them. And now I hope—I've been praying, actually—that they never do. That they never change their minds and decide to come for Mason after all."

"Rafe says there's no indication that they've been looking for you or Mason, or that any of them have scheduled trips to Seattle. He also said that he and Ian checked in with Smith—our cousin has repeatedly turned down the Bentleys' offers to invest in his movies because they always seemed smarmy to him."

She was clearly very glad to hear both of those pieces of news, but he could also see that when she looked back at the party, still in full swing, it was the last place she wanted to be. "I know I just got off the phone with your mother and we were planning to stay out later for our first official date, but—"

"I want to be with Mason now, too." He needed to hold both of them in his arms tonight and give thanks that he'd found them—and they'd found him. "We've spoken to more than enough people on my brother's behalf tonight. Let's go get your son and go home."

CHAPTER EIGHTEEN

They spent nearly an hour at Dylan's parents' house playing with Mason while he showed them the new toys Claudia had picked up for him. Max Sullivan was there, too, and though he was a man of few words, Grace could easily see how much he enjoyed her son as well.

Surprisingly, by the time they got back to her apartment, Mason was still awake. Not so surprisingly, he was in Dylan's arms, laughing at one of his silly faces. She'd never had a first date like this one, where they almost hadn't made it out of her apartment in the first place because they were so tempted just to jump each other instead. And she'd never spent so much time with any of her dates' families, either. But instead of feeling like Dylan's family were intruding on her time with him, she'd had a great time with Adam at the museum and then with Claudia and Max at their house.

"Your dad reminds me so much of mine. A man of few words, but all of them wise. Or funny," she added with a grin. She'd felt so safe with the Sullivans. Safe and—though she'd only known them a short while—appreciated. "Do your parents know the whole story about my ex, too?"

Dylan shook his head. "Only my brothers know. I was afraid that if I told my parents—"

"They'd end up worrying too much about us," she finished for him. "Now that I'm a parent, I get it. No matter how much you try to tell yourself that everything will be fine, you can't stand the thought of your own child ever getting hurt in any way."

When Mason wiggled, Dylan put him down on the floor, where he immediately crawled over to the coffee table to pull himself up.

"Look at you," she said. "What a big boy you're turning into." She turned to Dylan. "Why don't I brew us some coffee?"

But Dylan didn't reply. Instead, he was staring at Mason in amazement.

When she turned back, she saw that her son's little fingers were gripping the edge of the coffee table. Mason had a look of great concentration on his face, and Grace held her breath as he suddenly let go of the table and took one wobbly step and then another. Halfway into his third step, he fell with a plop onto his bottom.

He looked up at her and then Dylan as if to say, *Did you see me? Did you see what I did?*

She was laughing and crying at the same time as she swooped him up into her arms. "You walked!"

"You're amazing, kid," Dylan said, as much awe in his voice as had been in hers.

She had rained kisses over her son's entire face by the time he wiggled back down to the floor. He pulled himself up on the side of the couch and then, with a shove, propelled himself forward again.

Without thinking, Grace reached out to hold Dylan's hand. Or maybe he was the one who reached out for her. Either way, all that mattered was that he was here to share this milestone with her, and that he was as amazed by it as she was.

"We have to call your mom, have to take a video and email it to her so that she can see what Mason is doing!"

Dylan didn't seem to think it was at all strange for her to think of his parents when she and Mason had only just met them the week before. Probably because he knew his mom would go crazy over this news.

He filmed first Mason alone and then both of them when Grace held out her arms and Mason walked into them. She was so happy, even though she couldn't stop crying. But it was okay. She knew Claudia would understand, because Dylan's mother had likely cried tears of joy at all of her children's first steps.

Finally, Mason stayed on his bottom and started yawning and rubbing his eyes. "Looks like it's time to finally wind down for the night." It had been an incredible evening, and she knew she shouldn't be disappointed that it was over. "I should get him changed and into his jammies and then read him his usual bedtime story."

"My nieces and nephews tell me I do a pretty good job with bedtime stories," Dylan offered.

She was sure she'd never smiled so widely before or felt so happy in all her life. "In that case, we'll be right back."

* * *

Dylan's voice was so soothing as he read to Mason that Grace felt her own eyelids grow heavy. And maybe she would have fallen asleep if she hadn't been so totally sure that tonight was *the* night.

From their first kiss—heck, from the first time she'd set eyes on Dylan, if she was being totally honest with herself—she'd been on the verge of giving herself to him. And every time they were together, she moved closer to that daring tumble.

But when he'd rejoiced with her over Mason taking his first steps?

No woman could have resisted a man like that.

Though Mason began to make cute little snoring sounds partway through the story, Dylan didn't stop reading. With his attention on the book, Grace took the opportunity to feast her eyes on him, and to marvel yet again not only at how good he was with her son...but also at the precipice on which they stood tonight.

Soon the book would be put down, Mason would be in his crib, and there would only be the two of them.

Finally, Dylan shut the book and looked down at the little boy sleeping so trustingly, so peacefully, in the crook of one of his strong arms. When Grace saw the emotion in his eyes, she felt her own grow wet.

She'd tried so hard to be careful, to protect both Mason and herself from having a man drop into their lives and then drop out on a whim. But how could she ever have been prepared for a man like Dylan Sullivan? For his heart-stopping, infectious grins. For the serious way he took his boatbuilding work and his life's passion for sailing. For his strength, both in the way he used his hands and muscles to make a huge boat take shape, and in his personal convictions. For the gentle way he held her and Mason. For the way his family had taken in her and her son without so much as a pause. And, most of all, for the way he continually made her face her fears, one after the other. She hadn't nearly faced them all yet, but at least she'd finally stopped feeling like a shell of the old Grace Adrian.

"We never make it to the end of the book, either." She ran her hand over her son's soft hair. "I'll put him in his crib."

"Could I?"

Her heart should have been used to the way it always thudded like a rocket against her breastbone whenever Dylan was near, but she wasn't sure she'd ever get used to being with someone so selfless, so full of kindness—all of it wrapped up in the sexiest package imaginable.

She'd already let her son and Dylan laugh together, little manly in-jokes that had clearly filled her son's heart with pure joy. And she'd just let Dylan read Mason's bedtime story with her little boy on his lap. Shouldn't she draw a line—shouldn't she remind both of them that for all he'd played the part of Mason's father all night, he *wasn't*?

The way Dylan softly said her name told her he'd just read every one of her thoughts and could clearly see how torn she was about letting him even more deeply into their lives. Perhaps it shouldn't be such a big deal who put her son into his crib, but for Grace, that final kiss good night was a symbol of parenthood that she'd earned not just in every moment that she'd carried Mason inside of her body, but during every day of the past ten months when everything she'd done had been for him.

"I would protect Mason with my life," Dylan said softly. "If he ever needs me for any reason, I'll drop everything for him."

And that was when she knew she'd never have to worry ever again about her son where Dylan was concerned. Because even if the gorgeous man sitting beside her on the couch grew tired of her, she now knew with utter certainty that he'd never walk away from Mason. Her romance with Dylan had absolutely nothing to do with the bond the two of them had created with one another.

Her relief was so swift and heady that the smile she gave him was completely genuine. "I'd love it if you'd help put him to bed."

They walked together through the small living room and into the bedroom that she and Mason shared. His crib was in the corner, the stuffed zoo animals on the mobile above it sent dancing in the wake of the door opening. The changing table was beside it, loaded up with diapers and skin cream and wipes.

Most men, she imagined, wouldn't be particularly interested in baby things. But she could see how charmed Dylan was by the scene. At least, right before he turned to look at her bed and then at her as though he couldn't stop picturing the two of them having wild and crazy sex in it.

She'd been thinking of anything but sex when she'd bought the double bed and the sheets for it upon moving to Seattle. But suddenly, she knew she'd never be able to look at her bed in that sexless way again.

"Lucky guy," he said as he lowered her son carefully into his crib with a soft kiss to his forehead, "getting to share a bedroom with the prettiest girl in the world."

As soon as Mason felt the mattress beneath him, he turned onto his stomach and curled into a little ball with his butt up in the air. "That's his favorite way to sleep," she whispered to Dylan as she bent over the crib and gave Mason a kiss good night. "I love you, sweet pea."

Dylan reached for her hand and slid his fingers through hers before whispering, "You're lucky, too. So damned lucky to have him."

Any other guy she dated would probably have been beyond irritated that she shared a bedroom with her kid, but Dylan wasn't like anyone else, was he?

"I know," she agreed.

Mason's eyes came half-open, and he peered at them as if trying to figure out whether it really was bedtime or if he should get up again to play with his new favorite playmate, so she quickly led Dylan out of the bedroom.

He drew her into his arms as soon as the door closed behind them with a soft click and she had checked the monitor in the living room to make sure it was turned on. "I had a great time with you tonight. With both of you." His dark gaze was far more intense than his words would have indicated. "And I'm really glad you let me read his bedtime story tonight and put him to bed."

"I had a really, really good time, too. Just like always. I'm so glad you were here with us tonight."

"I am, too."

"Watching Mason take his first steps completely erased how sick I felt over what you told me at the museum."

"It helped me, too," he told her. "More than you know."

"It's been such an amazing night...I don't want it to be over yet."

Dylan didn't say anything in response, simply looked into her eyes as if he was not only trying to make sure she wasn't just saying what he wanted to hear, but that she truly meant it.

"*Stay.*"

The word came out as barely more than a whisper, which wasn't right. Not when she wanted him to stay with her tonight more than she'd ever wanted anything. It didn't matter how quickly her nerves had risen, or that she was trembling against him. She needed him to know how much this night had—and would—mean to her.

"Please stay and make love with me, Dylan. I know we've only got the couch, but—"

"The couch is perfect," he said as he stroked his hands down her back to the curve of her hips. "And don't forget the kitchen table." He shot a glance at the small rug in front of the gas fireplace. "The rug doesn't look too bad, either. And that's just the first three times."

She laughed the way she knew he'd intended her to, and also heated up the way he clearly wanted her to, as well, from his wicked suggestions of all the places he wanted to take her.

She wanted him in all those places, too.

"You're nervous," he said, his voice gentle despite the heat that remained. "Tell me why."

She was continually surprised by how much Dylan saw, and how deeply. After meeting his mother, his father, his siblings, she knew she shouldn't be so surprised. But he was just so different from any other man she'd been with.

And still...instead of truly being able to appreciate it, and him, she found herself always holding her breath, waiting for the other shoe to drop. Which was why it was more than just the physical aspect of their lovemaking that had her insides spinning. Tonight had to be about total honesty between her and Dylan. Honesty might have been only one of the many things that had been absent between her and her ex, but it had been the most important.

"*This* is what I swore to myself I would never let happen again. *This* is what I've fought so hard against for the past year and a half." She swallowed hard. "But instead of keeping strong, I just asked you to stay the night with me. I just begged you to make love to me. And the worst part of all is that if you were to leave right now, I'd feel emptier and more alone than I ever have before."

"I'm not going anywhere," he promised her, and the answering relief that swept through her made her knees nearly as weak as his kisses had. "You are the strongest person I've ever met, Grace. I know what a risk you're taking on me tonight after the way you've been hurt. I know you would never give yourself to a man if you didn't trust him. To know I've earned even a little of your trust, even if I don't have nearly all of it..." He smiled down at her as he brushed the backs of his knuckles across her cheek. "I'm nervous, too."

His confession stole what was left of her breath, especially because she knew he wasn't just saying it to try to make her feel more at ease by putting them in the same boat.

"Why?" She covered his hand with hers and drew it down so that his palm rested flat over her heart. "Why would *you* be nervous?"

"Do you really want to know?"

She would have said a quick and easy *yes* were it not for the fact that he was looking at her in a way that no other man ever had. She'd thought she was nervous about sleeping with him, but now she was a thousand times more nervous about his answer.

And yet, just as she couldn't have pushed out of his arms and asked him to leave, there was no way for her to pretend she didn't want to know his *why.*

"Tell me," she whispered.

His mouth curved up, just enough for his eyes to crinkle at the sides. "I'm in love with you, Grace."

Hadn't she known it was what he was going to say? Hadn't she read the truth of it in the way he looked at her? In the way he touched and kissed her? In the way he treated her son as though he was the most precious child in the entire world?

But that didn't make the impact of his words of love any less forceful.

The only way she could keep her legs from giving out beneath her was to grip his hand still pressed over her heart, while his other hand on her hip held the rest of her steady. She knew he could see how much he'd just rocked her world, even more than he'd already rocked it by simply existing. And yet, just as he'd always gently pushed her to let him into her life since the day they'd met, he didn't let her retreat from what he'd said now, either.

"I'm so in love with you that in one week, you and Mason have already become everything to me." He leaned in so that his cheek pressed against hers and his lips were at her ear. "That's why I'm nervous—because I want tonight to be perfect. Completely perfect."

His breath was warm on her sensitive skin, but she shivered at the beautiful things he was saying to her.

Beautiful, but so incredibly overwhelming.

Could she trust that what she felt really was love this time? Or was it just a deeper physical hunger than she'd ever thought to feel? And when would she stop being so frightened of making another mistake?

Grace had never been more grateful for anything in her life than she was for her son, but at the same time, she'd never withstand the kind of heartbreak she'd been through with his father again.

"I didn't tell you I'm in love with you so that you'd feel you had to say it back. I know I've pushed you to date me since the moment we met, and I can't regret doing that when I really do believe that you and I and Mason belong together. But I would never push you to give me your heart before you're ready, just as I would never push you to make love with me if you're not ready."

She wanted to tell him that he had her heart, wished she could just leap without being afraid of crashing and breaking into so many pieces this time that she'd never be whole again. But for tonight, there was only one thing she was one hundred percent sure about.

"I want to make love with you, Dylan. More than I can remember ever wanting anything else."

The final word had barely fallen from her lips when his mouth came down on hers, hot and borderline desperate.

"You can't want it more than I do." His lips rained a sizzling and heated path from her mouth to her jaw. "When does Mason wake up in the morning?"

She couldn't get her head around his question for a few seconds, not in the wake of the sensual pleasure of having his mouth and hands roving hungrily over her. Finally, she managed, "Six."

"How am I going to fit everything I want to do with you into nine hours?"

A rush of need hit her then, so potent that she went a little crazy. Crazier, even, than she'd already been for Dylan. Now that she'd decided to make love with him, to finally give in to the soul-deep craving that she'd been working so hard to fight these past weeks, need clawed at her. And she couldn't wait another second.

Grace reached for his shirt, her fingers fumbling and desperate as she tried to get it off him. "I need you to take me. Now. Right now."

She barely had his shirt halfway up when he put a hand over hers. "We may only have nine hours, but a little foreplay and a handful of orgasms aren't going to kill you."

A handful of orgasms before he finally took her? She'd never survive it.

"You know I haven't had sex in forever, that I haven't ever had it with a man who makes me feel the way you always do. Don't make me wait. We can just do it once to take the edge off and then—"

His mouth on hers cut her off, and though his hand fisted in her hair, the slow, sweet way his tongue stroked over hers until she had no choice but to match his rhythm told her more clearly than any words would have that he was most definitely going to make her wait.

And that she was going to love every single second of it.

CHAPTER NINETEEN

Dylan wanted to rip off the pretty dress that had been giving him little glimpses of cleavage and leg all night as she moved. He wanted to devour her in one big greedy gulp. He wanted to claim her and make her his own and never let her go. But even as desire raced through his veins so hot and fast that it nearly stole away his sense of right and wrong, he knew he couldn't let himself do any of that tonight.

Tonight wasn't about speed. It wasn't about taking.

It was about giving Grace endless pleasure.

Pleasure that would make her head spin so fast, she'd have no choice but to hold on tight to him...and never let go.

He slid his hand down to cup the nape of her neck. "Do you have any idea how much I want you? How many times I've dreamed about being inside of you in the past week?"

"Please," she begged again, "stop talking to me like that. You're only making it worse."

"Better," he promised. "I'm going to make tonight better than anything you've ever imagined."

He moved his hands so that he could slowly brush both thumbs over the slim straps of her dress on each shoulder, touching both fabric and skin. Though she was so hot to the touch that he felt scalded by her, she shivered.

"Your skin," he said as he lowered his mouth to press a kiss to one shoulder, "it's so soft. So sensitive. And so damned sweet."

He brushed aside the pretty braided fabric so that he could close his mouth over her collarbone. He loved the way she arched into him to give even more of herself than he was already taking. He'd meant it when he said he was going to kiss every inch of her that he uncovered. And as he made his way to her other shoulder and had to stop to lick into the hollow of her throat, her taste was so intoxicating that it was going to take everything in him to hold on to his self-control tonight.

"*Dylan.*" He could feel her nipples beading hard against his chest through her dress as she pressed herself tightly against him while working to take in a ragged breath.

He gave her more of what she clearly wanted by tasting the upper swell of her breast on the way to her other collarbone. She didn't say his name again, just made sexy little sounds of need and desire as she arched into him and silently begged him to take more of her.

All of her. That was what he wanted. Every perfect curve. Every beautiful, shuddering breath. Every sweet moan of desire. And even after they were temporarily sated from their lovemaking, he knew he'd want even more. *Everything.*

But for tonight, he'd have to be happy to take only what she offered. A few perfect hours with her naked and soft in his arms. A night he'd yearned for since the first moment he'd set eyes on her.

He lifted his mouth from her skin and made himself shift back. Just enough for her dress to slide even lower down her chest. "This picture," he said in a voice that was already raw with need, "of you standing here in front of me with your dress coming away, knowing you're going to be all mine soon—I'm going to replay it inside my head forever and ever."

She inhaled a shaky breath, one that shook her rib cage so that her dress slid even lower. "I will, too. The way you're looking at me, as though I'm..."

He lifted his gaze to her face. "*Beautiful.* You're the most beautiful woman I've ever seen."

He slid his hands back into her hair and pulled her flush against him so that he could devour her. She matched his passion with her own, quickly taking them closer to the edge than he'd meant to go.

"God, you tempt me," he said when he finally managed to draw back. "Do you have any idea how hard it's been to think straight around you when you're asking me your interview questions? If I've sounded like an idiot, now you know why."

"You've never sounded like an idiot." For a moment she looked a little nervous again, but then she slowly smiled. Such a sexy smile that he couldn't drag his gaze from the upturn of her lips as she said, "But since I love knowing that I've been tempting you all this time accidentally, how about I tempt you some more on purpose?"

His synapses tried to fire, tried to connect the dots of what she'd just said, what she'd asked. But before any of her words could string together inside his brain, she was taking a step back and shimmying so that the top of her dress finally slipped all the way off to pool at her waist. Leaving her clad only in an extremely translucent lace bra, pink with white trim.

Every muscle in his body tightened as he fought the urge to pounce. To rip her bra and dress off the rest of the way. To drag her down onto the rug so that he could claim her again and again and again until he had taken at least the edge off his desperation.

Though he'd sailed through plenty of storms with steady nerves, when he reached behind her to undo her bra clasp, his hands were shaking slightly and it took him more than one try to actually get it unhooked. It didn't matter how many times he saw Grace naked, he simply wasn't prepared for her mind-blowing beauty.

She sucked in a breath when he cupped her bare flesh. "The way your big, tanned hands look over me..." She shuddered in his hands, her eyes closing as he slid his thumbs over the taut peaks. "You know that handful of orgasms you said you were going to give me tonight?" He brought his hands down more firmly over her so that her nipples were rubbing against his palms. "I can't believe it, but I'm almost there already just from this," she confessed in a breathless voice.

But he could damn well believe it because he'd seen, again and again, just how naturally sensual she was, the most innately sexy woman he'd ever known. The way simply brushing a fingertip across her lower lip or rubbing his thumb inside her palm could make her pupils dilate, her skin flush, and her breath come faster. He hadn't missed one single sign since the day he'd met her, even if she'd mistakenly thought that her libido had died when her last relationship had gone so horribly awry.

He didn't give her any warning as he lowered his mouth to one breast. Her eyes flew open and her hands clutched the back of his head as if to keep him right where he was until she was ready to let him go. But she needn't have worried about him going anywhere, not when he could easily have spent the rest of the night worshipping her breasts.

He swirled his tongue over the tight bud of rose-colored skin and groaned his pleasure when he moved to lave her other nipple the same way. But it wasn't enough to go from one to the other—he needed to have more, to taste as much of her as he could have at the same time. Cupping her breasts in his hands, he pressed them together so that every kiss, every scrape of his teeth across her nipples, came right on the heels of the one before it.

They were still standing, but as he took her closer and closer to release with nothing more than his hands and mouth on her breasts, he could feel her grow less steady in her sexy high-heeled sandals. Intending to carry her over to the couch, Dylan swept her up into his arms, but she felt so good there that he couldn't bear to move just yet. Her lower lip was slightly swollen from where she must have been biting it when he'd been teasing her breasts, and her mouth drew his like the strongest magnet ever made.

When her hands wound around his neck while he kissed her, it meant everything to him that she was trusting him to make love with her tonight. Especially when he knew it was so much more than she'd ever intended to trust him, or anyone else, with.

A part of him wanted to kiss her until sunrise, to just keep teasing and taunting and tasting her perfect lips for hours. But he'd waited too long for this night—a week that had felt more like a lifetime—to rein in the need to get her completely naked and feast on the rest of her skin the way he was devouring her mouth. Without breaking their kiss, he carried her over to the couch, and when he laid her down on it, he went to his knees in front of her.

Looking at her lying on the couch—her full breasts bare, the skirt of her dress hiked up to mid-thigh, her hair across the pillows tangled from his hands, her mouth and skin flushed from his kisses—Dylan's heart nearly stopped in his chest.

"I could stare at you all night and never quite believe you're real." He whispered the words with more reverence than he'd ever felt for anything, even the ocean lit up beneath a full moon.

"I feel the same way—as though I might wake up soon and realize that it was all just a dream." She pressed her mouth to his, soft and sweet, before whispering, "It isn't, is it?"

"God, no." And as he took their kiss deeper again, he had to fill his hands with her, one sliding up the silky skin on the inside of her thigh, the other cupping her breast and teasing her nipple until she was arching against him.

It nearly killed him to lift his mouth and hands from her, but her dress was tangling on his fingers. "I need you naked. *Now.*"

When he reached for the zipper at the side of her dress and began to pull it down, he knew the sound would be forever connected in his brain with sex. The hottest sex of his life. Grace lifted her hips so that he could pull her dress down, and soon she was left wearing only sexy panties that matched the bra he'd already stripped away. Slowly, so slowly that he knew it just might do them both in, he slid the sheer panties off her hips and down her beautiful legs. Her breath came in hard pants as he moved his hands back up her legs, from calves to knees and then thighs before he finally—*finally!*—cupped hot, wet flesh.

She moaned as she shifted her hips up higher into his hand, and Dylan could feel how close to the edge *he* was. Too close. So close that he was afraid he might not be able to form a coherent thought soon. Before that happened, she had to know, "If you need me to slow down, if you feel like we're pushing too far, too fast, if you need me to stop, I will. No matter what."

"I know you will. That's why I don't want you to hold anything back from me. Not tonight. Don't hold back, Dylan."

With her words—*Don't hold back, Dylan*—playing over and over inside his head, he put his hands on her legs and dragged her hips to the edge of the couch so that her sex was just inches from his hungry mouth, with only her super-sexy golden heels still on.

"I can't hold back," he told her, every word raw, desperate, and totally honest. "Not with you."

God, she was sweet. And so damned addictive that as he tasted and teased the slick skin between her legs, though she definitely wasn't trying to get away, he gripped her hips tightly to hold her right where he wanted her. From the way her eyes darkened and her skin flushed even further, he knew she liked the slightly rough play of his hands over her soft curves.

Because for all her professed early nerves, Grace had always been one hundred percent sensual woman in his arms. And the way she gave herself over to pleasure as he slid one finger into her, then another, all while flicking the center of her arousal with his tongue? It only confirmed yet again that they were not only meant for each other, but also that her innate sensual hungers matched his perfectly.

One wicked image after another flew through his brain. Binding her wrists and ankles with silk ties to drive her to the edge again and again until neither one could take it anymore. Having her wait for him on her hands and knees for just long enough that she thought she might go crazy waiting even another second, then driving into her so that she came the moment he took her. Taking her out onto his boat, both of them naked as they dove into the water and then wrapping her all around him as she held on to the ship's ladder and he drove up into her.

Dylan had never wanted anything as much as he wanted Grace to feel good, so when she went tumbling into climax with his mouth and hands on her, he made sure to take her back up to the peak again before she'd even come all the way down.

"Dylan, I can't—" she began in faint protest.

But he could feel how close she was to coming apart again, less than sixty seconds after her first orgasm, so he replaced his tongue with his fingers. "One more. For me." Shifting so that he could kiss her mouth while still playing with the hot, wet flesh between her legs, he thrust his tongue against hers with the same rhythm as his fingers inside her.

Within seconds, she was riding his hand without any inhibition, and he nearly lost it, especially when he let himself think about the fact that soon it wouldn't be just his fingers inside her. He loved the way she was gripping his shoulders so hard that her nails scored his back, loved knowing that she'd marked him in her passion.

Marked him as *hers.*

She was soft and boneless against him as he came up onto the couch and gathered her close. She rested her head in the crook of his neck as he stroked her back while she worked to catch her breath.

"I thought you were kidding when you said you were going to give me a handful of orgasms," she whispered.

He whispered back, "Two isn't a handful."

Her eyes flew open again, and she might have tried to tell him she didn't have another orgasm in her for the night had he not covered her mouth with his. He was about to pull her up to straddle him on the couch when she beat him to it.

They were both panting by the time she lifted her mouth from his and said, "Who said the handful has to be all mine?"

"Grace..."

But she only laughed when he growled her name in warning, and when she yanked at his dress shirt, this time he didn't stop her from unbuttoning it partway and pulling it over his head. The sooner he was naked, the sooner he'd be inside of her. And once he was there, he already knew he'd never want to leave, never want to let her go, never want to stop loving her.

She lowered her mouth to his pecs, and again and again she kissed him, teasing and tasting him the way he'd teased and tasted her bare skin, until his head was spinning and he was gripping her hair in his hands the way she'd gripped his when he'd been loving every inch of her.

Drawing deeply from a bank of superhuman self-control, he lifted her back up over him so that they were mouth to mouth, chest to chest, hip to hip. "One more time, Grace. Come for me one more time before I make you mine."

He said the words between kisses against her neck and breasts, and when he slid his fingers back inside of her, he didn't let her set the pace this time, just took her up—up—up— so fast that all she could do was give both of them another climax.

She was so beautiful as she threw her head back to ride it out all the way that Dylan realized he'd never truly known just how powerful sex could be until tonight.

Until Grace, when his heart was just as bound to her as his body.

Certain that he'd finally wrung out every ounce of her pleasure, he reluctantly moved his hands from her damp skin so that he could kick off his trousers and boxers and pull a condom from the back pocket before throwing his clothes across the room. Seconds later he had the condom on and her waist between his hands as he lifted her up and over him.

But instead of driving into her the way he wanted to, he held her there, poised directly over him. He'd never wanted anyone, or anything, this badly, but he would never forgive himself for letting desire override any lingering fears she might still have.

"Grace?"

"We're protected?"

He nodded, knowing how important this would be to her, that no matter how much she loved her son, she would instinctively be worried about lightning striking twice and ending up pregnant again by accident. "Yes. I'll always take care of you, Grace."

She put her hands on his face and kissed him, so softly that she took him by surprise when she began to lower herself onto him. There were no words to describe how good it felt as she slowly enveloped him, nothing he could do anymore but tangle his hands in her hair as he took their kiss deeper.

Finally, they were pelvis to pelvis, chest to chest, mouth to mouth. Together, they rocked with each other, hard heat and soft flesh coming together in a perfect dance of pleasure. From moment to moment they took each other higher and higher until he was swallowing her gasps as the tight clasp of her inner muscles climaxing drove him all the way into his own release. One that crashed through him with the strength of a tsunami.

Again and again he thrust up into her, and again and again she came down over him, moving with such obvious joy that the waves took him completely under. Deeper beneath the surface than he had ever gone before. Deeper than he'd even known he could go.

Dylan could feel Grace's heart beating hard and fast against his as they held each other so tightly that there were no spaces left between them. Right here, with her, was where he always wanted to be.

Forever.

CHAPTER TWENTY

Grace had never known that she could completely lose herself in another person and just want to stay lost forever and ever. Was it because Dylan loved her? And, despite all the ways she'd tried to protect her heart, had she fallen in love with him right back?

"I want to stay with you tonight," Dylan said. "I want to hold you all night long."

Her ex had never stayed. He'd always said he needed to get back to the city to prepare for an early morning at the office, and she hadn't pushed, hadn't made him tell her the real reason he was leaving. She hadn't wanted to hear the truth that he had someone else or that she didn't really matter to him.

"I want you to stay, too." But that wasn't the full truth, and after what they'd shared tonight, she couldn't live with anything else. Not when even the smallest lie felt as though it would strip away the beauty of what they'd just done together. "But it scares me how fast we're taking *slow.* After tonight, it feels more like warp speed." Even that wasn't everything, though. "And I don't want to fix myself, fix what happened, with sex. Because what if that's what I'm doing?"

"If sex helps," Dylan said, "if making love with me makes things better for you, then I can't see why there's one damn thing wrong with it. There's nothing wrong with talking through pain, so why would it be wrong to kiss through it? To let pleasure strip away everything that should never have been there in the first place?"

"I never thought of it like that before."

"I haven't ever really had to fight demons of my own, Grace. But yours—I want to take them on headfirst, want to vanquish all your dragons with you, want to fight every battle beside you."

"Why?" She still couldn't see. Couldn't understand why he would give so much of himself—and his *love*—to her.

"There have always been two loves for me—my family and the ocean. And now, my heart is with you and Mason, too. I know telling you I love you isn't going slow, but I can't change how I feel. I love you, Grace. And I love Mason, too. More than I've ever loved anyone else."

The simple way he said it again and again, as if loving her and Mason was the most obvious, natural thing he'd ever done, shook her as deeply now as it had the first time he'd said it.

"Is it that easy?" She'd always needed to ask questions, always needed answers. But never more than she did right now. "Can you really just fall in love with someone and then, suddenly, they're your new number one?"

"Isn't that exactly what happened with Mason? Whatever other loves there were for you, they all got in line behind him."

"Yes." He was right. Exactly right. *Again.*

Grace was reeling from all of it. From her first official date with Dylan. From finding out that her ex had a string of paid-off women behind him. From watching Mason take his first step. From the most explosive—and tender— lovemaking of her life.

And now, from hearing Dylan tell her just how much he loved her in a way she hadn't known a man could express his love. Even her father, who had loved her mother dearly, had never been so eloquent.

One part of her wanted to push him away so that she could be alone to try to process it all. The other part never wanted to let him go.

"It's a small couch," she finally said.

"Good."

And when he slipped her heels from her feet and drew her against himself, her back to his front, cradling her head on his arm, she felt safer—and more cherished—than she ever had before.

* * *

Sometime in the middle of the night they reached for each other, kissing in the dark. Grace felt as though she were dreaming as she wrapped her arms and legs around Dylan and he came back into her, having already taken care of protection in the dark. And yet, there wasn't anything slow, or safe, about the way they took each other this second time.

How could there be when their hunger for each other hadn't been even the slightest bit sated by their earlier lovemaking?

He slid his fingers through hers, and she held tightly to him as he took her fast and hard over first one peak and then the next without any breathing room to recover. After so long a sexual drought, Grace felt utterly, wonderfully submerged in heady pleasure. She wanted to stay right where she was forever, holding on to Dylan's strong muscles in the dark, his mouth on hers as they both fell over the edge together.

And after, it was so wonderful to curl her body into his, to pull his arm over her chest so that she was holding his hand right over her still quickly beating heart, and to fall asleep safe and warm and, for the moment at least, sated from soul-deep pleasure.

* * *

Grace woke to the sound of Mason laughing. She knew how lucky she was that he usually woke up on the cheerful side of the bed, happy and excited to greet the new day. But today, she was momentarily lost as to why she was out on the couch instead of in the bedroom with him.

As the cobwebs cleared, flashbacks to the night before came one after the other. Kisses. Caresses.

And whispered promises of love from Dylan.

Her chest tightened where joy should have bloomed instead, and damn it, she was *tired* of it. Tired of being so wary all the time, of looking for trouble around every corner. So incredibly tired of not knowing anymore how to let go outside of Dylan's arms.

When, she wanted to know, would it be okay to just relax for a little while? And to believe, again, that true love could not only be real, but last forever?

Her parents had had such a sweet love and so did Dylan's. She saw that same love in the lives of his brothers Rafe and Ian, and his sister, Mia. All around her were examples of what was possible.

And yet, even though she wanted so badly to believe, she could still feel the scar tissue deep inside from a wound that hadn't yet fully healed.

Dylan, fortunately, knew that she was still healing and seemed to understand exactly why she was so wary, so cautious. He didn't try to pretend it wasn't the case, didn't try to fool himself into thinking that she could declare her love for him as quickly as he had for her.

But would he continue to be this patient? Or would he, if she couldn't rise above her past fast enough, finally give up on her?

Shivering at the thought of losing someone who had so quickly become the sunlight around which her world revolved, she wrapped the blanket around her naked body and let laughter draw her into the bedroom.

Perhaps after the night they'd shared wrapped up in each other, kissing and touching each other, she should have been better equipped to deal with the sight of Dylan wearing only dress pants, barefoot and shirtless, his face unshaven and scruffy—and looking more gorgeous than ever. She had to put her hand on the doorknob to steady herself for a moment as she watched the most sinfully good-looking man in all creation laugh with her son.

And for now, at least, the shadows that had begun to creep in couldn't withstand the bright joy of the two people who made her the happiest as Mason reached out to kiss her just as Dylan kissed her, too.

CHAPTER TWENTY-ONE

Grace was sitting behind her computer while Mason napped the next day, staring at the blinking cursor, trying really, really hard not to miss the man she was writing about, when the phone rang and she saw an unfamiliar number appear on the screen. Dylan had left the day before for Australia and the big, week-long yacht race. He had been as reluctant to go as she and Mason had been to kiss him good-bye, but if things were ever going to have a chance of working out between them, they would have to learn how to give each other the space they needed: Dylan for his boats, and Grace for her writing. This trip would be good for them, she reminded herself as she looked at the number on the screen and tried again to place it.

She'd never been nervous about picking up the phone before leaving D.C. But it was times like this when she immediately thought about her ex and his family and wondered if they had been tracking her after all—if they knew she'd had the baby and now were calling to try to take away her son so that he could continue the Bentley line.

As she let the call go to voice mail, she told herself as she had so many times before to stop looking for danger around every corner. She was just overtired from not getting enough sleep the night before. Not, of course, that she would trade the hot lovemaking with Dylan for any amount of sleep. Some things were *well* worth losing sleep over, she thought as a small smile moved onto her lips.

Yet again, even without being here, he was making her smile, making her forget the darkness that had so often felt as though it were lurking, waiting to pounce when she was at her most vulnerable.

Feeling much more steady, she hit the Play button on her phone and was surprised to hear a familiar voice. *"Hi, Grace, it's Tatiana. I hope it's okay that Dylan gave me your number. Since Mia surprised us all with a wedding, I wanted to surprise her with a party to celebrate it—just the girls. I know this is short notice, but is there any way that you'd be available to come by the set of my movie tomorrow night at six? Can't wait to hear from you."*

Even though Grace already knew how nice and down-to-earth the other woman was, it didn't change the fact that Tatiana was still a *massive* movie star. She couldn't believe that she'd just been invited to the set. Especially when she wasn't at all certain that she counted as "one of the girls" even though she'd been at Mia's wedding.

Not wanting to be rude, however, Grace called back immediately. "Thank you so much for the invitation to Mia's party. I'd love to come," she said honestly, "but I don't know if I'll be able to get a babysitter."

"Sorry," Tatiana said, "I'm a little fried from the scene I just shot today. I think the director actually wants to scrape off a piece of my soul for this movie." The other woman let out a long breath that Grace could easily sympathize with, given that she was feeling just as fried from trying to write her cover story about Dylan. "I also meant to say in my message that you should definitely bring Mason. Some of the other girls will be bringing their kids, too, and I know he'll have a ton of fun playing with them."

Grace had left behind everyone and everything she'd known a year and a half ago, which meant that she hadn't gone out for a drink with any girlfriends in a really long time. Suddenly, a night with the Sullivan women felt like exactly what she needed, even if she still couldn't quite shake the feeling that she didn't really belong in their league. Then again, she wouldn't ever have believed that she could end up with a man like Dylan...and look what had happened when she'd finally let herself go with him: *magic.*

"Count me in. Is there anything I can do to help set up?"

"Nope, I've got everything covered here. Just bring yourself and your cute little boy. And plan to have fun!"

* * *

Grace's evening was full, just as it had been for the past ten months, with feeding Mason dinner, then giving him his bath, reading him a story, and putting him to bed. But their bedtime ritual seemed a little bit off. And she knew why: It wasn't just that Mason's second tooth had just come in, it was also because they were clearly both wishing Dylan was there with them. Reading Mason a story. Kissing him good night.

And then holding her tight all night long after making the sweetest love imaginable to her.

Unfortunately, though it was late by the time she finally got Mason to settle down, since she was still struggling with her writing she returned to her computer to put in a couple more hours before she turned in. Forcing herself to hold focus on her article, rather than daydreaming about the main subject's kisses—or letting herself worry that something bad might have happened to him because he hadn't yet called—she began the heavy lifting of revising what she'd written earlier in the day.

Before she could make much headway, though, her phone buzzed and her heart leaped in her chest when she saw his name pop up on the screen.

Grace had promised herself she wouldn't stare at her phone all night waiting for Dylan to call. There had been too many nights when her ex had promised to check in, but hadn't. She'd believed Richard when he'd told her it was because he'd been working late and lost track of time—when, she later found out, he'd been courting the woman he actually planned to marry. Grace had simply been a convenient, and easy, bit on the side.

But Dylan had kept his promise, just as he'd kept every other promise he'd made to her so far. It had been a long time since she'd let herself feel the joy of wanting someone, and being wanted right back. Just as she'd relished the glorious hours in his arms two nights ago, she decided it was okay to relish this lovely warm feeling in her chest right now.

"Hi."

"Have I mentioned just how much I love the sound of your voice?"

Just like that, he had her flushing, heat moving through her. "It's really nice hearing yours, too. How was your flight?"

"Good. Although I may have driven myself a little crazy thinking about you the whole time. I'm so glad you're still up. Once we get going tomorrow morning, it might be hard for me to catch you again, so I really needed to talk to you tonight. Tell me about your day."

"Tatiana called and invited Mason and me to a surprise party for Mia that she's throwing on her set."

"My sister is going to love seeing both of you again. And Mason is going to dig playing with my cousins' kids. Just don't let any of the girls corrupt you. Especially my cousin Lori. She can be a wild one, particularly when she and Mia get together." Grace was amazed, yet again, by how easy he made things sound, as though he wasn't surprised at all that she'd been invited to a big family party when they'd only just started dating. "How's your writing going?"

She knew better than to bother with a *good* this time. "I'm going to get it soon. I just know it. And until then, I'll just keep plugging away at my computer so that when lightning strikes, I'll be ready."

"Next week on Sunday," he reminded her. "Once we get you out on my boat, it's all going to come together for you."

Her heartbeat kicked up even faster at the thought of sailing with Dylan, just as it always did when she thought about being alone with him in his ultimate domain. Right there in the cockpit confessional.

"What about Mason? I've been missing that little guy like crazy. How was his day?"

"It was great. His second tooth finally popped through."

"Every day there's something new and exciting, isn't there?" Dylan truly sounded interested and excited by this small milestone. "We'll have to celebrate his new tooth when I get back."

Dylan's reaction reminded her of how her parents had raised her, where even an event as small as her baby growing another tooth was something to celebrate.

Thinking about how Mason had been a little off all day, she said, "He misses you." But she knew that was cheating. Dylan had given her his all since they'd met, and he deserved better from her. "I've been missing you, too."

"You have no idea how tempted I am to catch the next plane back to you."

"You've got to do this race," she told him. "And you've got to promise me that you'll enjoy it." She'd never forgive herself if she and Mason stole Dylan's truest joy from him.

"I'll trade you that promise for one from you." The tenor of his voice had shifted as he spoke, from playful to sensual.

"What do you want me to promise you?"

"That we won't hang up tonight until you've come for me."

"But—" She could hardly speak around the desire already rising inside of her. "How can I do that when you're not here?"

"Promise me, Grace."

Shocked by how close to the edge nothing but the sexy promise in his voice had taken her, she whispered, "I promise."

"All day long I've been putting together a fantasy about you in my head. Will you help me live it out?"

"Yes."

God, yes.

CHAPTER TWENTY-TWO

"Where are you right now?"

"Sitting at the dining table behind my computer."

"Put your computer away and go over to the couch."

Grace's hands were trembling as she followed his instructions. "I'm on the couch now."

"Tell me what you're wearing."

"A long-sleeved T-shirt and jeans."

"*Everything* you're wearing, Grace."

The sensual command in his voice—one that had shocked her in the best possible way when they were making love—sent a rush of heat to the tips of her breasts and between her legs. "I'm wearing lingerie I think you'd really like."

"I like them all," he said in a raw voice that perfectly backed up his claim. "What does it look like?"

"Sheer white lace. Pink silk trim. Similar to what I had on Wednesday night underneath my dress."

He groaned. "You're so beautiful, you blow my mind. Can you put the phone on speaker without waking up Mason?"

"If I keep the volume down low."

"Good, because I'm going to want you to be able to use both hands."

Now she was the one groaning. "Dylan—"

"God, I love it when you say my name like that. Like you're dying for me to touch you."

"I am. I want you so badly."

"Take off your shirt and imagine my fingertips grazing your skin, and then my lips when I can't keep my mouth off you."

She lifted up the cotton. But where it should have been the same thing she'd done a million times before, tonight she couldn't get the image of Dylan taking it off out of her head.

"Tell me what you see, what you feel. Every detail."

She'd never done this with anyone else, never played a sexy game of pretend on the phone. Had always assumed that she'd be too embarrassed to be able to get into it. But Dylan made it all seem so easy, so natural.

"I'm breathing faster already, just from dreaming of having your hands on me, and knowing that's just the start of all the amazing things you're going to do to me tonight."

"Oh baby, you have no idea."

She could have stopped there, knew he wouldn't push past her limits, but she wanted to know that she'd made him feel just as good. "The sound of your voice, the feel of your hands on my skin—they've made my breasts so sensitive beneath my bra."

"Jesus." He blew out a breath. "That's the hottest thing I've ever heard in my life. That I've ever seen. Touch yourself, Grace. Touch your breasts."

"Through the bra...or out of it?"

"Keep it on for now. Tell me how it feels to have the lace scratch against your beautiful nipples."

"Good," she said on a gasp of pleasure. "So good."

"Bare. I need you bare now, need to see, need to touch, every inch of your perfect breasts."

She reached for the clasp of her bra. "I'm taking it off right"—she clicked it open—"now."

"I'll never be able to hear that sound again without getting hard. Are you touching yourself?"

"Yes." She was whispering again, just loud enough for him to hear. "My breasts feel so full, so sensitive, like all you'll have to do is run your tongue over me and I'll explode."

"Do you want me to be gentle tonight, Grace? Because I'm feeling pretty damn desperate, and I don't know if I can control myself too much longer."

"I love it when you're gentle," she told him, "but I also love it when you can't help yourself and get a little rough."

"Touch yourself the way I would if I were there with you right now. Like you've already made me lose control."

She closed her eyes, and when she imagined Dylan's hands on her, a little rough and desperate with desire, a new rush of heat flooded her. "I love it when you start to lose control. It feels so good."

"You have no idea how good it feels," he told her. "I could play with your breasts all night long. Would you want that, Grace? Would you want my hands and mouth on you for hours and hours?"

"*Please.*" She was nearly whimpering by now.

"Soon," he promised, before saying, "now I want you to run your hands down over your ribs and stomach, appreciating every inch of your gorgeous body the way I would if I were there with you."

She'd always been on the curvier side, and from the first moment Dylan had looked at her, and then when he'd touched her, she hadn't had to doubt just how much he loved her body. "You always make me feel so beautiful."

"The most beautiful woman I've ever seen," he confirmed in a deep voice that resonated with need. "Undo the button on your jeans and then lower the zipper."

The sound of the zipper coming apart had Dylan groaning again. "You have no idea how hot it is hearing that and knowing sheer lace is showing through. Tell me what you're doing now. Are you touching yourself? Or are you waiting for me to tell you to do it?"

She knew by now how amazing, how hot sex with Dylan was when his hands, his mouth were on her. But what he was able to do to her with just his deep, sexy, hungry voice?

She could hardly breathe, hardly think, she wanted him so much.

"I want to touch myself so badly," she admitted. "I *need* to. But..."

"You know that the anticipation of waiting for me to tell you to touch yourself will make it even better."

"*Yes.*"

"You make me happy, Grace. So damned happy."

"You make me happy, too." She was half naked on her couch having naughty phone sex...and she was smiling so big her cheeks hurt. "Really, really happy."

"How about I make you even happier by telling you to take off your jeans now. But leave the white lace on for a little while longer."

"Okay," she said a few seconds later, "my jeans are off."

"I'm taking a mental picture of you right now, lying on your couch, almost naked, wet and ready for me." A low sound of pleasure rumbled from his chest through the phone. "*Perfect.* God, you're *perfect.*" She thought she heard his zipper come down, too, then, but before she could ask, he said, "I want you to slip your hand inside your panties."

She had to bite her lip to stifle her moan of pleasure as he finally instructed her to touch herself. "I'm inside."

"Jesus, Grace, you almost made me lose it." She could hear his breath coming faster and loved knowing that she could make him lose control. "Tell me how you feel. I need to know how hot, how wet you are for me."

"I've never felt like this before," she told him. "Like I can't wait another second or I'll go crazy."

"Just a little longer," he urged her. "Just wait a little longer, and I promise I'll make it good for you."

"I know you will. You always do."

"Slide the lace down your legs now. Do it slow and easy, even though I know you want to tear it off just like I did the first time we were together on your couch."

She truly did want to tear her panties off, wanted any barrier between the two of them gone, but she followed his directions, made herself go slowly.

"Are they gone? Are you completely naked now?"

"They are. I am." Her words were shaky. "Please, Dylan. Don't make me wait any longer."

But instead of telling her it was finally time to let herself go over the edge, he said, "Run your hands up from your thighs, to your hips, then over your breasts."

Every inch of her was so incredibly sensitive by now that even the slightest scrape of her nails over her skin had her gasping from sensation.

"If I were there with you right now, I would follow the path of your hands with my mouth. I'd kiss and lick and bite my way up your body and then back down between your legs until you were screaming my name. And you'd taste so good that I wouldn't stop with one orgasm, I wouldn't stop with two—I'd take you over at least three times before I'd move back up your body again."

She could barely stop from screaming his name now. "I'm so close, Dylan. I don't know if I can hold on any longer."

"I love you, Grace." He paused just long enough for his beautiful words to sink in before adding, "Now come for me."

She had barely touched herself when her back arched up off the couch and soul-deep pleasure exploded inside her.

"That's it," he ground out, his own breath sounding as fevered as hers. "Don't stop touching yourself, don't stop making those beautiful little sounds. I'm right there with you." He uttered a low curse, one that vibrated through every inch of her in exactly the same way it did when he was hard and hot inside of her rather than nearly eight thousand miles away.

"*Dylan.*" Knowing that he was also touching himself, that he'd leaped off the peak with her, had her spiraling back up and into another climax.

Neither of them spoke for a minute or two as they worked to catch their breath. She felt too wonderfully spent to bother with putting her clothes on, so she simply reached for a blanket.

"Did you like that?"

She took the phone off speaker and held it against her ear, as though that would bring Dylan closer. "I *loved* it."

She could practically see him smile through the phone. "You keep blowing my mind, Grace."

"I might even have blown mine tonight," she teased, barely stifling a yawn halfway through.

"You've had a long day. I should let you go to bed."

She wanted to stay on the phone with him for hours, but she knew both of them needed clear heads tomorrow. He had a week-long race to start in his friend's boat, and she had a story to nail before she went to Mia's surprise party.

"I love you, Grace. And if I can't reach you again for a few days while I'm racing, I want you to promise me you won't forget it."

I love you, too, she thought. *I love you so much.* The words were on the tip of her tongue, playing over and over in her head so loudly that she half-thought he'd be able to hear them. But in the end, all she managed to say was, "I won't forget, Dylan. I promise."

"Sweet dreams, sweetheart."

"Sweet dreams."

* * *

Grace's thoughts were jumbled as she put the phone down. If anything should have been "just sex," it was what they'd just done. And yet, it had been so beautiful. So emotional.

From the first, she'd known Dylan Sullivan was special. He made her feel things no other man ever had. And yet, she'd still been determined to deny it, to hide from it. But Dylan had been equally determined not to let her keep doing either one. Slowly, patiently, he'd touched her heart just as gently, and as thoroughly, as he touched her body.

She'd taken that first scary step toward something real by letting his brother Adam know that they were no longer just interviewer/interviewee, but were dating. That had been frightening enough. Still, she'd told herself that just because they were officially dating didn't mean they wouldn't still be taking things slow.

But tonight she could no longer deny what she really felt—and had felt almost from the first moment that Dylan had taken her son in his arms to calm his crying. A love that had already grown big. Strong. And undeniable.

She'd been close, so close, to saying the three little words aloud on the phone tonight. But something had held her back at the last second. The fear that once she let herself believe, truly believe what they were building could last, it would all be ripped away from her.

To let herself love Dylan Sullivan with all her heart and then lose him?

Oh God, it hurt even to think of it.

She'd been a wreck after her ex had dumped her, but it hadn't been because she was heartsick. It had been because she was disgusted with herself for being stupid enough to fall for his act. And after she'd vowed to protect both Mason's and her own heart, she'd told herself the two of them didn't need anyone else, that they were already a perfect little unit. That determined independence had gotten them across the country and settled into a new life in Seattle.

But now...what if she truly opened up the door she'd locked down so tightly a year and a half ago? What if she decided to stop being so wary? To trust that Dylan meant it when he said he saw the three of them together forever? And to finally let him in so that her tight little unit of two became three?

Of course, she already knew that opening a door for Dylan Sullivan actually meant pulling down an entire wall for his whole family. A big, wonderful family who had taken them in from the very first moment.

Grace had been raised by two wonderful parents who had always taught her to look for the good in people. Yes, she'd been burned. Badly burned by her ex and the other Bentleys. But they hadn't destroyed her or Mason. Hadn't even come close.

She'd trusted before, and with Dylan's help—and his love—she was learning to trust again.

She nearly called him back, but she wanted to see his face when she finally said the three words she knew he'd been hoping to hear, wanted his arms around her when she risked everything by saying *I love you.*

* * *

Dylan's body was loose after the hottest phone sex in history, but his mind was racing so he grabbed a beer and stepped out on the deck of the waterfront condo in which his friend was putting him up for the night before they got out on the racing yacht.

All day long, he'd been thinking about Grace. When would she accept her feelings? When would she trust him not to ever hurt her in any way? And when could he finally claim both Grace and Mason as his own?

He'd called her without video because he'd wanted the intimacy of fantasy, the thrill of pretend, to be what drove them both over the edge. But even more than he'd wanted to be there with her tonight watching her skin flush and her eyes darken with desire as he made love to her, he wanted to see his ring on her finger. He wanted Mason to officially be a Sullivan. And he wanted to know that both of them were forever protected from anyone in the past who might try to rise up to hurt them.

He'd texted his brothers to set up another meeting as soon as he returned from the race. This time, everyone would come with what they'd learned about the Bentleys to work out their game plan. Because in the same way that Dylan had had the sixth sense that his life was going to change right before Grace and Mason had shown up at his boathouse, his gut was now telling him that the wind was shifting again, quite possibly bringing a tornado this time.

Dylan looked out over the Sydney Harbor, one he'd sailed many times in the past few years. He was looking forward to getting out on the water and breaking another record this year. But he was looking forward to getting back to Grace and Mason—the woman and child who were already and would forever be *his*—a hell of a lot more.

CHAPTER TWENTY-THREE

Grace had planned on working for a couple more hours the previous night after getting off the phone with Dylan. But, utterly and blissfully exhausted, all she could manage was to crawl into bed to rewind and replay every moment of their super-sexy phone call.

When Mason had awakened her this morning with his usual cheer, she'd felt just as happy. *It's because both of us are in love with Dylan*, she thought as she lifted him out of his crib with a smooch. Every moment they'd spent with him was full of joy, full of laughter.

And full of love.

She was tempted, again, to call Dylan so that he would finally know the truth of what was in her heart. But with his race starting today, and the seventeen-hour time difference, she probably wouldn't be able to reach him. Plus, it would be so much better to look into his eyes and hold him close when she told him how much she loved him. That she'd never loved anyone the way she loved him. That he made every day better and better.

And that right when she thought love had ended, it had only just begun.

She changed Mason, then brought him out into the kitchen and clipped him into his high chair to feed him breakfast. He mowed through mashed peas, carrots, and a huge handful of Cheerios. When he stopped eating and began to toss the leftover cereal at his stuffed animal in the toy box in the corner of the living room, she quickly cleaned him up with a wet wipe and then let him loose to play.

Playing that quickly turned into more awe-inspiring walking.

It took her longer than she expected to finally sit down at her computer to check her email, where she found a message waiting from her editor. Her deadline was still two weeks away, but he wanted to see something soon so that the art department could begin working on the layout of both the article and the cover, for which they would shoot the photos upon Dylan's return from Australia.

Grace's heart immediately started knocking around in her chest. She'd never been this nervous about something she'd written before, even during the past year and a half when it had been a struggle to get the words down. Writing about Dylan was so personal, so close to her heart, that she wanted it to be perfect. Needed it to be the best thing she'd ever written.

Dylan had augmented her great research with the best one-on-one interviews a journalist could dream of from her subject. All of the pieces for this story should have been there. But when she opened up the file again and read through it while Mason banged cars together on the floor, then toddled over them like a baby Godzilla, she couldn't deny that something was still missing.

She replied to her editor's email to let him know that she would be sending something over very soon, then settled Mason into his bouncy seat in the bathroom and took a quick shower. With Mia's surprise party that afternoon, buying a present for it, and figuring out what to wear, she wouldn't have time to work on her story again until tonight. Considering she'd redone the beginning a dozen times already, it was probably a good thing that she was getting away from her computer for a while so that she didn't butcher the story by rewriting all the life out of it.

Because if there was one thing that she knew for sure, it was that her story about Dylan Sullivan should be as fun and as full of joy as the man himself. Anything less wouldn't do him—or what he'd accomplished—justice.

* * *

Several hours later, Grace walked onto Tatiana Landon's movie set holding Mason in one arm and a pretty wrapped gift in the other. She'd interviewed actors and actresses before, but no one of Tatiana's caliber. The set was very impressive, the furniture from the 1920s authentic down to the finest detail.

When Tatiana had told her that she was working on a period film—and that she was more than a little nervous about pulling it off—Grace had marveled at her bravery. Most actresses would likely be happy to stick to what they had proved they were good at. Tatiana, on the other hand, clearly thrived on the challenge of learning a new skill set and reaching outside of what she already knew how to do so well. Ian Sullivan, Grace remembered with a small smile, had been so proud of his fiancée. The way he'd looked at Tatiana with so much love that it stole even Grace's breath still stuck with her. It was the same way Ford had looked at Mia. The same way Rafe had looked at Brooke.

And the same way, she was finally ready to believe, that Dylan always looked at her.

"Yay, you're here!" Tatiana rushed over and gave both of them a hug. "Wow, look at how much you've grown since I last saw you," she said to Mason. "What a big boy you are!"

One day, Grace thought as she watched Mason smile shyly for the beautiful woman fawning over him, Tatiana was going to make an amazing mother. And Ian would be a great, and very protective, father. Just as he was a great, protective older brother.

"Mia isn't here yet. I told her to come in thirty minutes. She thinks I need her help with finding another location in Seattle for a new scene in the movie." Tatiana grinned. "She's going to be so surprised when she sees everyone."

"How many of Mia's cousins were able to come?"

"Everyone on the West Coast. I hate that I couldn't give enough lead time for the girls out in Maine and New York, but having everyone else and the kids here is pretty amazing. They can't wait to meet you."

What, Grace wondered, had Tatiana and Brooke told the other women about her? Especially since she and Dylan had only recently gone public with the fact that they were dating. Then again, hadn't they all known something was up from that first dinner at Claudia and Max's house?

Mason spotted the twins first, a boy and girl who looked to be just a little bit older.

"You must be Grace and Mason." The twins' mother had one of the friendliest smiles Grace had ever seen. "I'm Sophie, and this is Jackie and Smith."

Mason was already wriggling to get down with the twins. "Looks like he wants to play."

"I've set up an area over here for the kids with some toys so that it will be easier for us to keep an eye on them."

Of course, Mason made a beeline for a colorful little drum. Jackie and Smith picked up their own little instruments, and soon the three of them were delightedly playing a song together.

"Looks like they've decided to form a band," Grace joked.

"I should probably have left some of these noisy toys at home. But my kids really love them."

"So does Mason. The first time he met Dylan's mom, he immediately went to town playing drums in her kitchen with the pots and pans."

"Claudia told me how much she adores watching him."

"She's really great with Mason. Like the grandmother he never had." Grace hadn't realized the words were coming until she said them and flushed hot at the insinuation that Claudia would be playing that role with Mason soon. It was too close to everything her ex had accused her of when she'd told him she was pregnant. But Grace wasn't with Dylan so that she could become a part of his very important and wealthy family. She was with him because he made her happy. "I didn't mean to imply that she...or that I..."

Grace finally stopped trying to take her foot out of her mouth when she realized Sophie was grinning like crazy.

"After chatting with Claudia about you and Mason, I'm sure she'd be *thrilled* if you *did* imply it! But before I make you any more uncomfortable by basically trying to hogtie you and your son to Dylan, how about I wave over one of the catering staff for a couple of glasses of champagne?"

It was barely late afternoon, but Grace knew a little bubbly would go a long way toward easing her nerves. "I'd like that."

"I heard you're a writer?"

"Yes, I write freelance articles. That's how I met Dylan—I'm writing a piece on the heart of a sailor for *Sailing Magazine.*"

"I'm a librarian in San Francisco, so I'll make sure we have extra copies on hand for our patrons." A pretty brunette walked over with a small baby in her arms, and Sophie quickly made the introductions. "Megan, this is Grace. Her son, Mason, is playing drums with Jackie and Smith."

"It's so lovely to meet you," Megan said.

"You, too. Your baby is gorgeous." Grace moved closer so that she could better see his little face. "How old is he?"

"Logan is six weeks." Megan gazed down at him, love radiating from every part of her.

Just then a lanky blond girl who had to be around eight or nine ran over. "Mom, everyone is snarfing up my cupcakes like crazy! I told you I should have made more."

"Next time, we'll pack the car as full as we can," Megan promised. "Honey, this is Grace. Grace, this is my daughter, Summer."

"You're Dylan's new girlfriend, right? I've never seen him with a girl before. Are you going to marry him?"

Megan's eyebrows went up. "Summer, you can't say that to someone you've just met!"

"But Brooke and Tatiana were telling everyone that they've never seen Dylan so head over heels for anyone. Doesn't that mean they're going to get married?" Before her mother could reply, Summer said, "Oh yum, they just brought out tea sandwiches. My favorite!"

"I'm really sorry about that," Megan said with a little shake of her head. "She tends to speak without thinking sometimes, and she was just so excited that one of her favorite cousins is finally happy."

"Your daughter is great. You don't have to apologize to me for anything." In fact, Grace was thankful for what Summer had said, because now she knew exactly what everyone was saying. And while it scared her a little to think that Dylan had made his feelings for her that clear to his family, it also warmed her to know how special she was to him.

"Maybe I could make it up to you by letting you hold Logan?" Megan offered.

Grace eagerly held out her arms for the little baby wrapped in a soft, blue-and-green striped blanket. "Mason isn't even a year yet, but it seems like forever since he was this small. I've forgotten how tiny they are."

"And I've forgotten how much they eat and poop," Megan said with a laugh. "Funny how quickly our brains erase that, isn't it?"

It was true, Grace thought. For all the sleepless nights she and Mason had had in those early months, what stuck with her were the smiles, the cuddling, how much fun they had playing together, and the sweet way he always fell asleep halfway through story time.

An adorable toddler led a pregnant woman toward them by the hand. "Smith! Jackie!" The little girl waved at Sophie's kids. "I'm here!" A few seconds later she was giving each of the other kids a big hug, including Mason, who clearly loved being with them all. Grace laughed along with everyone else at the little girl's exuberant and very sweet greeting.

"I'm Chloe," the pregnant woman said, "and that whirlwind is Emma."

"I'm Grace. It's nice to meet you." Grace was glad she was meeting the women who were parents first, because at least it gave her something in common with them. If she had met one of the other famous Sullivans first, she would have been a lot more nervous.

"Look at how cute they are, all playing together!" exclaimed a petite woman with faint pink and blue streaks in her hair. "I've got to take some pictures to send to Marcus."

Speaking of feeling nervous, Grace immediately recognized Nico. A massive pop star, her songs were constantly on the radio. She knew she should stop being so gobsmacked, considering she'd already met Ford Vincent and Tatiana Landon. But, honestly, what struck her most of all was how *normal* they all were. Where were the massive egos? Where were the entourages?

As soon as Mason saw the other kids hamming it up for Nico, he didn't hesitate to get right in there.

"Is he yours?" Nico asked when she finally put her phone away.

"He is. He's Mason, and I'm Grace."

"It's great to meet you. I'm Nicola. And from what I can see, Jackie, Smith, and Emma have found their new BFF." She leaned over to give baby Logan a kiss before snapping some pictures of him, too. "I don't know how much more of this my hormones can take."

Megan shot Sophie and Chloe a quick look before saying, "Are you and Marcus thinking of getting pregnant?"

"I know we only just got married and I'm in the middle of a tour, but..." She looked back at the children all energetically playing their little instruments. "Every time I'm with you guys, I find myself thinking more and more about having kids. Plus," she said as her eyes got all dreamy, "Marcus is going to be an amazing father."

The women all nodded, with Sophie saying, "The best."

"I know there's no rush," Nicola said, "but I don't know if there's any reason to wait, either."

"You've got great instincts. You'll know when it's right for you," Megan said.

"Or maybe one day you'll just wake up pregnant like I did," Sophie said with a laugh.

A woman who was nearly a carbon copy of Sophie walked up just then and said, "You didn't exactly just *wake up pregnant.* I believe there was some wild sex during a one-night stand with a really hot guy first."

"Meet my twin, Lori," Sophie said to Grace. And then to her sister, "This is Grace."

"Ohh, you're *gorgeous*," Lori said. "No wonder Dylan is gaga over you."

"Lori and Summer share a lot of the same qualities," Megan said with a grin.

Grace knew she had two choices: Either feel overwhelmed by Dylan's family and bolt...or roll with it and just have fun. After little more than a week with Dylan, she knew exactly what the right answer was.

Fun.

"It's nice to meet you, too, Lori." Grace nodded toward the group of kids. "The toddler whaling on the drums over there is my son, Mason."

"Seriously, the two of you are perfect. Double-no-wonder my cousin is head over heels. Dylan is great with kids, isn't he?"

"He's certainly amazing with Mason."

"Dylan is only five years older than me and Soph, but when we were kids, he would come up with the most fun games. And," Lori added with a nod toward her twin sister, "he was usually the only one who could get her to stop crying."

Sophie rolled her eyes. "I was only crying because you were so loud all the time that you made my head hurt. Still are," she added with a smile. "Dylan's awesome with Smith and Jackie, too. Definitely right up there on their favorite-uncle list."

Just then, the lights started flashing. "Mia must be here!" Lori declared in a loud stage whisper, even though there was no point in trying to conceal themselves with the kids making so much noise.

"I'm so glad you could drop by the set today, Mia," they heard Tatiana say in a voice made deliberately loud enough to carry to everyone. "How was your honeymoon?"

"It was a week of sex and sleep on repeat with great food and plenty of tequila mixed in. What could be better? I feel like I could tackle pretty much anything now."

Grace's parents weren't prudes by any means, but she hadn't grown up with the subject of sexuality spoken about so freely, nor had a group of girlfriends who shared details. The thing was, instead of feeling uncomfortable about it, she found that she really liked it.

Why shouldn't sexuality be something to celebrate?

Lord knew she and Dylan had celebrated it last night over the phone...

"Oh good," Tatiana's voice carried over, "I'm glad you're not too tired, because...SURPRISE!"

They all called out the word a beat after Tatiana, and Mia looked truly stunned. "Oh my God, how did you pull this together without me finding out? I can't believe it. You guys have just made my amazing week even better!" She hugged one person after another as tears spilled down her cheeks. "I'm so glad all of you are here. Ford and I really wanted everyone at the wedding, but—"

"Ford is so famous and such a magnet for paparazzi and fans that you did exactly what you needed to do," Nicola said before Mia could apologize for anything. "And I, for one, think your surprise wedding at your parents' house sounds like the most romantic thing *ever.*"

"Me, too," said a woman with a long dark braid over her shoulder whom Grace hadn't yet met. "In fact, Zach and I are thinking of stealing the idea from you two."

"Ryan said the same thing," a blond woman said with a smile.

"But I love big splashy weddings," Mia exclaimed. "And I really want to go to both of yours."

Laughing along with everyone else, a woman whom Grace instantly recognized from her shopping trip earlier in the week as the owner of Indulgence said, "That's why we're having a big splashy reverse bachelorette party for you today."

Seattle had seemed so big, and she'd been so busy holed up with her computer and baby, that Grace hadn't been sure she'd ever really meet any women with whom she could connect. But now, all because of Dylan, she finally felt like all the pieces of her life that had been ripped apart were coming back together. Not only because she was finally letting herself relearn the pleasure of being part of a couple, but because these women were rounding out the other part of her life that had been so lacking since she'd left her friends behind a year and a half ago.

Grace had often wondered if starting over had been the right choice. Now, it looked like it was. Like she could leave her past behind and finally move on...into a new life that was so far beyond her wildest dreams that she knew she'd be pinching herself for a really long time, just to make sure she wasn't dreaming.

* * *

A little while later, Mason half-walked, half-crawled over from the group of children and reached for her. "Are you tired from all the playing, sweetie?" she asked as she lifted him into her arms. Compared to Megan's new baby, who had felt so small and light, Mason was an armful. One she never got tired of holding.

He laid his head on her shoulder and put a thumb into his mouth by way of an answer. She figured he'd probably take a little nap in her arms and then wake up starving. They could share a piece of Mia's delicious vanilla and raspberry cake, Grace decided.

She thought she saw a couple of camera flashes in her direction and assumed it must be Nicola still taking pictures as Mia moved beside her. "I'm so glad you're here."

"I am, too. And I have to tell you, again, just how beautiful your wedding was. The best I've ever been to."

"The tabloids are freaking out about how we could possibly have gotten married without anyone knowing about it," Mia said, clearly happy about thwarting the paparazzi. "And since we were having sex twenty-four seven and didn't come out of our suite in Hawaii, they couldn't get any shots there, either."

"I can't imagine how hard that must be."

"It's not always fun. But if pushy journalists are the worst thing that comes with being with Ford, I'll take it." Grinning, she said, "Speaking of *awesome* journalists, Ford and I both read a bunch of your work in Hawaii. You're really a great writer." Before Grace could thank her, she asked, "How's the story about my brother going?"

"It's getting closer." At least, she hoped it was, given that her editor needed to see something soon. "We're going sailing a week from this Sunday when he gets back from Australia. He's convinced that will put the missing pieces into place."

Mia raised her eyebrows. "He never takes the women he's seeing out on his boats." Dylan's sister looked extremely pleased by this information. "That's how I knew he was never serious about any of them. Because he never wanted to share the most important part of himself with a woman until now." She smiled at Grace. "Until you."

CHAPTER TWENTY-FOUR

All the next week, though the demands of his round-the-clock racing and the time difference meant that Grace and Dylan had continued to miss connecting over the phone, she still felt happier than she could ever remember being. Even the fact that Mason had been fussier than usual, because yet another new tooth was working to push through his gums, wasn't dimming the goofy smile she'd been wearing.

Ever since she'd realized that she was in love with Dylan, her work on the cover story had begun to flow. Better, at least, than before. The challenge now was for Grace to write about him without her piece sounding like a love story—something she was struggling with enough that she'd continued to hold off on sending her editor anything yet—especially given all the sweet surprises he'd sent her and Mason during the week he'd been away.

On Monday, she'd come home to find a package with Mason's name on it waiting on her doorstep. Inside was a brightly colored toy sailboat, perfect for bath time. Mason absolutely loved splashing around with the boat, and something told her she had a little sailor on her hands. *To celebrate Mason's new tooth. Give the little guy a kiss for me. Love, Dylan* was all the note that came in the box said, but it spoke volumes to Grace about the amazing bond that Dylan already had with Mason.

Tuesday, another package came, this one filled with homemade chocolate-chip cookies and chocolate truffles. *For extra writing inspiration, my mother's homemade cookies and Brooke's truffles. Love, Dylan.* She was beyond touched that he'd remembered her saying that chocolate always helped her with writer's block.

On Wednesday, she received a call from a nearby theater letting her know that there were two tickets waiting for her and Mason for a children's concert that she'd wanted to attend but that had been sold out for ages. Of course, they were the best seats in the house, and Mason had positively glowed with happiness as he baby-danced and clapped to the fun songs.

Thursday, she opened a beautifully wrapped package to find the silkiest, sexiest lingerie imaginable. His note—*To replace the pair I tore off. Love, Dylan*—made her feel hot and tingly all over.

And on Friday, in a thin overnight mail package, was one small piece of paper that said *I love you* in his strong, steady handwriting. Grace knew it would always be one of the most precious things she would ever receive.

Each of his surprises had been thoughtful and loving. But the best gift of all was knowing Dylan would be back today...and she couldn't wait to *finally* tell him that she loved him.

They'd agreed to take things slow, and at first she'd believed that would keep her safe from falling too fast, and too hard, for Dylan. But no rational plans could keep her heart on the slow-and-safe track when all it wanted to do was somersaults and cartwheels whenever he was near. Especially when he was kissing her and running his big, strong hands over her naked curves so that she was coming apart for him again and again.

Everything was finally falling into place.

All because of *love.*

As she put away the toys strewn across the living room carpet that Mason had tired of now that he was ready for his nap, she felt a heightened awareness of the way her sundress brushed over her curves. After chatting with Colbie at Mia's party, she'd learned that Indulgence was having yet another sale and, of course, hadn't had to have her arm twisted to stop by on her way home. She couldn't wait to see Dylan's face, first when he saw her in the new sundress...and then when he stripped her out of it and saw that she was wearing the lingerie he'd sent her.

It wasn't easy to stuff down her heady anticipation, but after she put Mason down for his nap, she needed to make some seriously good use of the next couple of hours on another small article that was due soon, in addition to the one she was writing about Dylan. She picked Mason up, and with her free hand, she clicked open the digital calendar on her phone to reconfirm her deadlines.

But when she looked at the dates, her stomach suddenly dropped.

Her period was supposed to have started the week before...and she was never late. In fact, the only time she'd ever missed it was when she'd been pregnant with Mason.

Grace didn't realize her hold had tightened on her son until he started whining and pushing at her arms. She looked away from the dates on her phone to Mason's upset face.

Nine months from now, was he going to be a big brother?

Joy and amazement hit her first at the thought of another baby. Dylan's baby. One who was sure to be a fearless and free spirit with a ready laugh, just like him.

But barely sixty seconds later, fear clawed into her system. So much fear that it edged the joy right out.

Mason began to squirm in earnest, desperately in need of a nap after the previous

night when he'd awakened every couple of
hours crying and gnawing on anything he could
shove against his gums. But she needed to know
immediately whether or not she was pregnant
before Dylan came home from his sail.

Would she soon be the mother of *two*
illegitimate children? Oh God...

The very last place Mason wanted to go was
into his stroller, and both of them were sweaty
and red-faced by the time she clicked the
buckles in place. It was never easy to get the
stroller down the small flight of stairs from her
apartment, but when he was wailing and trying
to get out, it felt nearly impossible. But she had
to get to the store, couldn't wait through his nap
and then a night with Dylan with the possibility
of pregnancy hanging over her.

Was it just yesterday that she had been
walking down this same street, enjoying people
watching and window shopping, feeling as if her
life might finally be heading down the right
track? Now, she didn't notice the sun sparkling
off the blue water, didn't see pretty dresses in
store windows or crave the fruit at the corner
stand.

Grace had never forgotten this feeling of
having her life change abruptly from one
moment to the next. Ten years ago it had
happened when her mother had passed away.
Two years ago it had happened again when her
father had died. Six months after that, it had
been when she'd learned she was going to

become a mother. And then, just weeks ago, she'd looked at Dylan for the first time and felt that same jolt of awareness that told her nothing would ever be the same.

Now, shockingly, there was a very strong possibility that everything was going to change again.

Grace all but ran down the sidewalk with Mason. She knew she needed to calm down, buy the test, and wait to see what the results were before she freaked herself out any more than she already had. But she was too tired, too stunned, to stop the what-if's and how-could-I's that were already spinning around and around in her head.

When she broke the news to Dylan, would he look at her with the same disgust and horror that Richard had? What if he thought this was what she did—find rich men to seduce and then "accidentally" get pregnant?

No. She wasn't making sense. She knew better than to compare Dylan with Richard. But with everything twisting up inside of her, she couldn't seem to stop the crazy thoughts from coming.

A gray-haired man held the pharmacy door open for her, and when she thanked him, her voice sounded thick and hoarse, as if she'd been crying. The chain store had the same layout as the one where she'd purchased the pregnancy tests back East, so she quickly wheeled to the correct aisle and picked up two new tests, the same brand that she'd used before. Feeling like her life had somehow gotten stuck on repeat, she took them up to the counter to pay.

When the woman at the register looked at the tests and then down at Mason, who had fallen asleep in his stroller, she beamed at Grace. "I had mine close together, too, and it was an absolute godsend! They were best friends, always there for each other, even now."

Grace knew better than to trust her voice again, so she simply nodded and fumbled for the cash in her purse, then left the store as quickly as she'd come. But the stranger's words had rent her utterly in two. Because, for as frightening and life-changing as it would be to have another baby in nine months, she could also see how amazing it would be for her son to have a sibling so close to his age. After all, look at Dylan and his brothers and sister, who were all so wonderfully close.

Grace was extra careful not to wake Mason as she carried him and his stroller up the stairs, but his eyes opened the moment she got inside. For the next thirty minutes, she tried everything she could think of to get him to fall back to sleep. Not only because she knew he still desperately needed the rest, but because the clock was ticking down and Dylan would be knocking on her door soon.

Finally, he lay peacefully in his crib, his breathing slow and steady as he cuddled his blanket and stuffed animal close.

It will be okay, she told herself as she took a moment to watch him sleep. *Everything will work out, one way or another.*

Grace closed the bedroom door with a soft click and was just about to pick up the plastic bag containing the pregnancy test when there was a knock on the door.

Oh no, Dylan was early! She quickly brushed her hands over her face and hair, even though she knew he'd take one look at her and instantly know something was wrong.

Working to draw from her newfound confidence, she took a deep breath and reminded herself that no matter what happened from here on out, she'd proved that she and Mason would be okay. They would not only survive, they'd thrive.

Without looking through the security glass, she opened the door. "You're earl—"

Her words fell away as she realized she wasn't speaking to Dylan.

"Hello, Grace." Richard Bentley smiled at her without so much as a shred of guilt or remorse. "I'm here for my son."

CHAPTER TWENTY-FIVE

Grace had played out this scenario a thousand times during the past ten months. Each time she'd thought about what would happen if Richard changed his mind about not wanting Mason, fear had skittered up her spine. But now that he was really here, all she felt was anger. Such deep fury that he'd dare to come and claim the son he'd walked away from without so much as blinking that she nearly slammed the door in his face.

But she knew she needed to think clearly, needed to make sure she learned exactly why he'd had a supposed change of heart, so that she could bolster her fight to keep her son from him. And she also needed to keep him physically as far from Mason as possible.

She stepped out on the landing in front of her apartment and closed the door behind her. "Why are you here?"

"I saw a picture of you holding a baby at a Sullivan party." On his face she could see the primal urge to claim his child now that he'd finally seen Mason's picture and knew for sure he existed. "Which one of the Sullivan men are you screwing to get an invite to a private celebration?"

There was a picture of her and Mason from the party Tatiana had thrown for Mia? Grace knew with perfect certainty that none of the Sullivan girls would ever pass on their personal shots to the press. Not when Mia, Tatiana, and Nicola already had to deal with far too much pressure from the paparazzi. Had one of the wait staff secretly taken pictures and leaked them? Was that what those flashes had been when she'd been holding Mason and speaking with Mia? And did any of the Sullivans know yet that it had happened?

Fear was trying to clamp around her chest, but she wouldn't let it. Wouldn't let anything rob her of the ability to think clearly.

"I'll bet you're doing the architect, aren't you?" Richard continued with a sneer. "I shouldn't be surprised you landed on your feet, given that seducing rich men is your specialty. Still, I didn't think you'd be able to get a Sullivan to fall for your tricks, especially dragging a baby around with you." He gave her his best threatening look. "I want to see him. I want to see my son."

By the barest of threads, Grace held back from punching him in the face. Not just for talking about her as though she were a slut with ulterior motives, but for daring to bring Mason into it. But she knew better—knew that if she so much as laid a finger on him, he'd likely call the police to have her arrested, and she'd be unable to protect her son while dealing with his charges.

"He isn't yours," she said first, knowing the truth of it all the way to the depths of her soul. "And he's at his babysitter's," she lied. "But that's irrelevant, given that you didn't want to see him before, didn't even want him to exist. What could possibly have changed?"

He'd looked so confident when he'd greeted her a few moments ago, but now she saw the first flicker of confusion cross the face she'd once been foolish enough to think was handsome. How had she not seen the weakness beneath the veneer of polish learned at the boarding school and Ivy League college his parents had sent him to?

"You've changed," he replied. "You used to be so—"

"Malleable? Naïve?" She shook her head. "All that changed the minute I realized what you and your family are really made of. What makes you think you have any right to come here?"

"I never thought you'd go through with it. That you'd actually have the kid on your own. But when I saw the pictures of you and him, I realized I already had the son I've been trying for with my wife—"

"And you suddenly thought you could change your mind? Well, you're wrong. You can't. You gave him up, and he's all *mine.*"

"You're just bitter because I didn't want you, because I didn't want to marry you and take care of you."

A couple of months ago, she might have let him convince her this was true. But now she knew better. So much better that she didn't even need to argue or to protest that it wasn't true. When he'd turned away from her when she'd first told him she was pregnant, she had been horrified to realize that he didn't want to know his child. Worse, that he'd told her to get rid of it without blinking an eye. But now she realized what a gift his disinterest had been, because Mason was a million times better off without the Bentleys in his life.

"You didn't want to take care of anyone but yourself," she countered. "Your name is nowhere near the birth certificate."

"I can easily get a DNA test."

"I suppose you could," she agreed. "Although I can't help but wonder how your wife feels about your plan." She could see that he was still confused about why she wasn't yet cowering or giving in to his demands. "Does she even know you're here?"

"It doesn't matter what she thinks. She'll do what I tell her."

"Even taking on another woman's child after she's 'failed you' by not being able to get pregnant?" But Grace didn't need to wait for his reply. "Actually, I'm sure she will, since that's probably how your entire relationship has been so far." Grace knew she shouldn't feel anything for Richard's wife, but how could she help but feel sorry for someone who was a part of that horrible family? "What about your parents? Have you consulted them about your change of heart?" He flinched, and she didn't care if it was small of her, she loved seeing it, enjoying his discomfort. "They wanted me and the baby even less than you did."

All this time she had thought she wasn't tough enough, wasn't good enough, but now she knew better. She was strong. She was good enough...and she wasn't putting up with her ex's crap for one more second.

"They want an heir to carry on the name," he told her, but she could see from the uncertainty in his tone and expression that he hadn't yet run his plans by the senior Bentleys. Which, on the plus side, meant that they hadn't personally sent him here to take Mason. "Now tell me where the babysitter lives so that I can go see my son."

"The day you offered me money to get rid of him, he stopped being your son." She knew it was finally time to play the cards she'd kept so carefully guarded just in case this should ever come to pass. And then, as soon as he got the hell away from her, she'd finally use her defense fund to hire the best custody lawyer to keep Mason safe. "I have proof that your parents tried to bribe me with fifty thousand dollars to abort the baby and then another fifty thousand to never speak of my time with you. I kept the checks they forced on me."

"This isn't over," he said, but even as he said it, she could see that she'd shaken his confidence. First by asking him if his parents—who kept him on a very short leash—knew what he was doing right now, and then by reminding him about the Bentley blood money. "My son is going to want to know who his father is. What are you going to tell him?"

"I won't lie to him. Not about you, or anything. One day, when he's old enough, it will be up to him if he wants to see you. But right now it's up to me. And I don't want you or your horrible family to have any part in his life." She moved closer to him, with enough fierce purpose that though she was nearly a foot shorter and he'd come here to intimidate her, *he* was the one taking a step back. "You are going to go away now and leave us alone. And if you come back at any point without my express permission, I will go to my extensive contacts in the press and expose you and your parents for the kind of people you really are."

He tried to stand his ground then, as he blustered, "Do you really think people will believe some slut who's just trying to get her fifteen minutes in the spotlight? Or are they much more likely to believe a senator? It will be your word against theirs."

She knew the word *slut* was supposed to hurt her, but she was bulletproof now. The scared girl who had broken down when he'd dumped her was gone, and in her place was a woman who would fight to the very end to protect the child she loved.

"Actually," she said in a remarkably cheerful voice, "it will be their word against *themselves.*"

"Bullshit. You have no proof that they did anything wrong. Giving you money to help you out is not a crime."

"When your parents came to my house, I was transcribing an interview. I had the recorder in my hand." She enjoyed watching the color drain from Richard's face. "They were so full of themselves that it never occurred to them that I would fight back, or that I would record their 'offer.' And you know how recognizable your father's voice is."

"I always knew you were trash," Richard snarled at her. "All it ever took to get you into bed was the price of a fancy meal and a couple of glasses of champagne."

She could have shot back a half-dozen barbs, but she was done with him. Completely done.

Besides, she knew that the reason he was trying to wound her now was because he finally understood that he couldn't fight her for Mason, not if there was a chance of the former senator's recording coming to light. Richard might not have known too much about her, but he clearly knew she wasn't a liar. She wouldn't make a threat like this if she didn't intend to back it up.

Still, Grace would make sure the legal pieces were in place right away so that she would be armed and ready to fight for custody just in case he tried to take her to court for parental rights.

"I've given you your one and only warning to stay away from us," she told him now. "And I wouldn't make the mistake of pushing me. I might have been a pushover once, but I'm not anymore. If you so much as try to contact either me or Mason again without my permission, I'm going to let the entire world listen to the esteemed former U.S. senator and his wife try to make absolutely certain that I didn't have the baby none of you wanted."

With that, she stepped back into her apartment and closed the door in his face.

The shaking didn't start until she tried to lock the door. It took her two tries to get the bolt into the slot, all the while thanking God that Mason hadn't woken up. If he had started crying while she was facing down her ex, Richard would have realized that she'd been lying about Mason being with a babysitter and might very well have pushed in to see him.

She'd dealt with Richard all by herself and knew she'd dealt with him well. But in the aftermath of the confrontation, Grace needed desperately to lean on someone, to know that she wasn't alone. Because even though she'd taken care of the situation with her ex, she needed Dylan. Not only to call him to tell him what had happened, but also to hear his calm, reassuring, loving voice before she got on the phone to do whatever it took to persuade the top child custody lawyer in the country to take her case.

Grace went to get her phone and that was when she saw the bag from the pharmacy sitting on her kitchen table. Oh God, how could she have forgotten?

She still needed to take the pregnancy test.

CHAPTER TWENTY-SIX

Dylan had been counting the minutes until he could be with Grace again.

If Mason was still napping, he figured they'd barely get the front door closed before her clothes were off and he was inside of her. Later, after they'd spent the rest of the day playing with Mason and then put him to bed for the night, they'd move to a slow seduction. One in which pleasure would spiral out for hours and hours.

But the second Grace opened the door, despite how incredibly beautiful she looked in her dress, all those fantasies disappeared. She didn't say anything, just stepped aside to let him in. When she closed and locked the door, her hands were shaking.

"What's wrong? Is it Mason? Is he sick?"

"No. Mason's fine." She put her hand on Dylan's arm before he could run into the bedroom to check for himself. "He's perfect."

Relief swamped him a beat before he realized that she wasn't speaking to him as though they were lovers. Or even friends. Instead, that wall she'd had up during their first interview was back. And she'd taken her hand off his arm too fast when she should have been pulling him closer instead.

"Talk to me, Grace. I can see that you're upset. What happened?"

Her face crumpled for a second before he watched her visibly work to pull herself together. "I was going through my calendar, looking at my deadlines, when I realized..." She looked up at him, the emotion in her eyes piercing straight through him. "I thought I was pregnant."

"Pregnant?" The thought of Grace carrying his child rocked his world so much that it took him a few seconds to take it in. "We're going to have a baby?" He hadn't seen this happening, but he was happy. Couldn't remember ever being this happy.

"No."

He was halfway to pulling her into his arms. "Wait. I thought you said—"

"I took a test. Two, actually. They're both negative. I'm never usually late, but maybe the stress of everything lately has made my system go off schedule."

Dylan knew he needed to control his disappointment, but he'd never lied to Grace before and wouldn't do it now. "Ever since I met you and Mason, I've wanted you in my life. I've thought about being his father a hundred times, but I never thought past that. Hadn't thought about you and I making our own baby together. But when you said that you thought you were pregnant, when I thought that it meant you were..." He drew her against him the way he'd been about to just moments before. "It was the best news I'd ever heard."

"How?" She looked utterly confused. "How could it be?"

"You make great kids, if you hadn't noticed."

"But we haven't known each other that long. I mean, I know we've had fun—"

"Yes, we've had fun. And I hope we always will. But what we are, what we have, is so much deeper, so much bigger and stronger, than just having fun."

She didn't pull away, but she wasn't putting her arms around him, either. "When I realized I was late, when I thought that I was pregnant again from out of the blue, I thought I had ruined everything. That you'd think this is what I do—I pretend to protest that I'm not easy, then go around sleeping with every successful guy I interview in order to reel them in."

He took her face in his hands. "I would never think that. It doesn't matter how long we've known each other, how long we've been dating. I knew you were the one the second I saw you. Both of you. You're it for me, Grace. And," he added with a grin, "if you wanted to try to change the results on the pregnancy test for next time, I'm all for it."

But instead of the answering smile he hoped for, she still looked as serious as he'd ever seen her. "What else is wrong? It's not just thinking you were pregnant, is it?"

She took a deep breath, one that shook in her chest. "The party I went to last week for Mia at Tatiana's set—some pictures leaked from it. I don't know who could have taken them, maybe one of the wait staff? All I know is that there was one of me and Mason."

"Your ex," Dylan instantly guessed. He had to work to keep his hands from fisting at the thought of the bastard coming after her and the baby. But it didn't work. Couldn't work when the fear that something bad might happen to them was the worst feeling he'd ever known. "He saw the picture, didn't he?"

"I was freaking out thinking I might be pregnant when I heard the doorbell ring and thought you were back early. I couldn't believe it when I saw him standing there. Not just because he'd managed to track us down so easily, but because I couldn't believe he had decided he wanted Mason after all."

Fury continued to rise swift and hot within Dylan as he said, "He doesn't deserve one damned minute with Mason."

"That's what I told him—that the second he told me to get rid of the baby, he ceased to be his father. Richard thought I was going to be afraid of him. He thought I'd just give in. He thought I was still the naïve girl who had fallen for him without looking deeper than the fancy dates, the pretty words. But he was wrong."

Looking at Grace, listening to her paint a picture of the showdown, Dylan could see exactly what her ex had faced: the fearless fire in her eyes, the determination to stand strong in every line of her face and body.

"He never knew you at all. Never knew one damned thing about you. You're one of the bravest people I've ever met. And when it comes to your son, you'll do anything to protect him. Only a massive idiot wouldn't understand that— or someone who is too self-involved to pay attention to anyone else."

"I still don't know how I didn't realize that about him, that all he cared about was himself. What he wanted. His own image. Taking whatever he wanted from whomever he wanted without ever giving anything back, while convincing himself that he was a great man because he gave away family money that he never had a hand in earning."

Dylan was glad, frankly, to hear the anger in her voice after what she'd had to face today. Anger would help keep her strong for the time being. And it was a hell of a lot better than being afraid.

"He knew his parents had tried to pay me off, of course. Knew all about their untraceable checks, because mine wasn't the first they'd had to hand out, as Rafe discovered when he investigated him. But Richard didn't know everything, couldn't have known I recorded my entire conversation with them."

Despite everything, Dylan couldn't hold back his smile at how clever she was. "You *recorded* them?"

"I was doing some transcription from an interview that day they came to see me. They didn't see the recorder in my left hand. The former senator's voice is extremely recognizable. So I knew that if I ever had to protect myself from them, the recording would do it."

"I love you, Grace. So damned much, it blows my mind." He kissed her then, partly because he could never resist her beautiful mouth and partly because he needed to reassure himself that no harm had come to her. "You scared the crap out of him, didn't you?"

"I'm pretty sure I did. And I'm going to hire the best child custody attorney to make sure that they scare him, too. I've been saving up for this. I have a legal defense fund ready to go."

"I'm sorry I couldn't head him off at the pass, Grace," Dylan told her. "Lord, I wish I had. My brothers and I, we were going to meet tomorrow to figure out what to do to make sure something like this never happened. But we were too late, and you ended up having to face him alone." And he'd spend the rest of his life making this up to her. "Rafe deals with broken families all the time, so he'll know who the best custody lawyer is to make sure you and Mason never have any problems with the Bentleys, no matter what they might try to pull in the future. I'll call him right now, have him shoot you to the top of his firm's priority list."

She had closed her eyes for a moment, and he could see how pale, how shaken she still was. He was rubbing his hands down her arms, when she opened her eyes and looked into his.

"Thank you, but this time I need to do it myself. All by myself."

"You're one of us now—"

"No, I'm not," she said in a voice that was becoming more and more shaky by the word. "I can't do this." Her eyes filled with tears. "I thought I could, but I can't." The tears began to spill. "I'm sorry, but I just can't."

CHAPTER TWENTY-SEVEN

Everything inside of Dylan clenched, then froze. "You've had a crazy day, Grace. You don't have to do anything more, don't have to make any big decisions. Not tonight. Not after you've just been through the wringer on all fronts."

"I knew all along that I should have tried harder to resist you. But I kept telling myself it was just one kiss. Just one night. Just one week. Just for fun. Just for pleasure." She wiped away her tears as she sucked in another shaky breath. "I've been lying to myself, and I can't lie to myself anymore, Dylan. I can't lie to you, either, by letting you think that I'm ready for this. For you."

"I promised you we'd go slow, Grace. I know I've pushed too hard from the beginning. Pushed you to meet my family. Pushed you to give me your days and your nights. Pushed you to let me into Mason's life. Even though I knew you weren't ready. You never lied, not once. I'm the one who's screwed up again and again. Let me fix this. I'll make sure you aren't roped into all my family's parties—"

"Your family is great. They've been amazing to me and to Mason."

"Then *I'll* back off. I'll give you space, all the space you need, let you dictate the pace of things from now on."

"Don't you get it?" She pushed out of his arms and spun away. "That's just the problem. I don't want any space! I want you all the time. *Every single second.* I've wanted you more and more since the first time I met you, the first time we spoke, the first time we kissed."

He didn't want to spook her any more than she already was, so he made himself stay where he was rather than go after her. "That's good, isn't it? That we both want the same thing?"

"No." She shook her head, frantic now. "How can it be good to feel so totally out of control with my body, my heart, my head, whenever I'm with you? Whenever I even think about you? How can it be good that I fall deeper and deeper for you every single moment? How can it be good that your family already feels like mine and Mason's? How can it be good that I want to lean on you for everything? For comfort? For pleasure? For safety?" But she didn't let him answer any of her questions, just zoomed ahead into more. "I was finally—*finally!*—feeling in control of my life again. And then you showed up, standing out in front of your boathouse looking gorgeous and perfect and reaching for Mason like you'd simply been waiting for the two of us to walk into your life."

He knew it might be the wrong thing to say to her right now, but anything else would be a lie. "I was waiting for you. For both of you. I've always been happy. Always loved my life. My family. But I knew there was a missing piece out there, a love and a family of my own, like my parents have with each other and me and my brothers and Mia. I knew I would find it one day, and then, suddenly, there you were. The missing pieces, right there in front of me. I fell in love with both of you that day, and every day since has only confirmed what I knew to be true in that first moment. You're mine, Grace. Both of you." He reached for her. "I want to be yours, too."

For a moment, as she looked into his eyes, he thought she would move into his arms and give him everything he wanted: *her love.*

But then her face was crumpling all over again, and she was moving back. Away from him, rather than closer. "I missed you when you were gone. Not just on this trip when you were racing, but after that first day we met in your boathouse, when you left to ferry the boat up north. Can't you see how screwed up that is, that I already missed you so much already when I hardly knew you?"

"I missed you, too, Grace. Missed Mason. What's wrong with that?"

"Everything! Everything is wrong with it. Of everyone in your family, you're the free one, Dylan. You're the one who has never been pinned down by anyone or anything. And no one has ever made the mistake of trying. Not when they knew that it would hurt you. What about when you want to go sailing or racing on a day I can't bear to let you go? What if you know I'll miss you too much so you turn down the chance and don't take the trip to the one place you've been waiting to see? You'll hate me for stealing your freedom."

"Never. I would never hate you. You're right that I've always been free to do whatever I want, to go wherever I want, to live life as an adventure. Now I want to live those adventures with you and Mason."

For a moment he thought she might let herself believe that what he was saying was really true, but then she shook her head. "I've seen how determined you are, the way you manage to move heaven and earth to turn your dreams into reality. And you'll never know how much I admire you for it. Or how much I wish I could be like you. But I've only just started to get my life back together. And I've got a baby to take care of, to find a playgroup for, to enroll into preschool soon. What if I let you give up your freedom for us and then the land starts closing in around you? What if you plan a trip, a badly needed sail so that you can reconnect with who you really are, and then it turns out you can't go because you have to be here for something with Mason? Then you'll resent us both."

"Grace—"

"Mason and I are just starting to set down roots. Roots we desperately need. Roots I would never forgive myself for if all they did was bind you up."

"The only thing I would ever resent," he told her, "the only thing that would ever make me upset, is losing you. Losing Mason. I'm ready for this, ready for change, ready to learn how to operate as three instead of just one." He prayed his heartfelt words were getting through as he said, "Being with you, having a child—or, hopefully, more than one—doesn't mean I'll never get out on the water again. Of course I will. With my wife. My son. A daughter, too, if we're lucky."

"You don't even know if I can sail," she protested. "Maybe I'll only get in the way out on the water."

"I've seen you navigate meeting my family. And today, the way you dealt so bravely, so brilliantly, with your ex. You'll be a natural out on the water, Grace. Mason will, too." He reached for her, pressed her hands to his chest, right over his heart. "Give us a chance to figure all this out together as a team."

"I wasn't supposed to fall for you." Tears were spilling down her cheeks. "It was just supposed to be me and Mason. I planned to do anything, everything, I could to keep him safe.

But then you came into our lives and turned everything upside down so fast. Too fast."

Dylan knew why she was reeling, understood that her ex appearing out of the blue combined with thinking she might be pregnant again had dragged up all of her fears, all of her worries, all of her trust issues. Especially when she already felt as though her feelings for him were spiraling out of her control.

But just because he understood didn't mean he wasn't beyond frustrated. He wished he could just keep talking to her until he'd convinced her to see things his way. But all he could do, for tonight at least, was draw her into his arms and hold her for as long as she would let him.

She didn't break down in tears again, simply held on tight as he felt her gather her strength. He didn't know how long they'd been standing together in the middle of her living room when Mason woke up, crying.

"I have to go get Mason." She had already drawn back from Dylan's arms, far too quickly for his peace of mind. "I got him down too late for his nap today and now everything's off."

Before, she would have invited him into the bedroom to soothe Mason. Would have let him lift Mason out of the crib and into his arms. But now, she was simply waiting for him to leave.

"Tomorrow," he said, desperate to know that leaving now didn't mean never seeing her again. Desperate to have some time to think of a way to persuade her to change her mind about taking a risk in loving him. "We were going to do the sail tomorrow. The missing piece for your story."

"Your mother was going to watch Mason, but now—"

"She loves him, Grace. You know that. Nothing that happens between you and me is going to change that. Let her watch him tomorrow while we go sailing."

Mason wailed again from his crib, louder this time, and the sound pierced Dylan's heart. God, how he hated not being able to go to him, to comfort the little boy whom he'd been praying would soon be his.

"Okay," she said quickly. "I'll meet you at your boathouse at three o'clock. But I need to get Mason now. And I want to make sure that I lock up behind you."

Which meant she needed him to leave.

But when she opened the door for him a few seconds later, even though he knew he had no choice but to go, there was something he needed her to know. "I told you before that I'd never experienced heartbreak, never truly regretted anything. But now I know that if you don't let yourself love me back, I'll finally be broken. And I'll never stop regretting losing you and Mason."

* * *

Dylan's phone was ringing on the front seat of the Jeep, where he'd left it. When he saw his brother Rafe's name on the screen, he immediately picked up.

"Richard Bentley is in Seattle," Rafe said without preamble. "I've called you a half-dozen times in the past hour to try to tell you. Where the hell were you?"

"With Grace. Dealing with the aftermath of his visit. He threatened her and tried to make her hand over Mason."

Rafe swore. "Is she—"

"She stood up for herself. She told him to leave her and Mason the hell alone and has leverage to make sure he does." He quickly told his brother about the recording and that he needed Rafe to get the best damned custody lawyer on board ASAP. "Where is the bastard staying?"

"You're planning to hurt him, aren't you?"

"Hell, yes."

Rafe could have told him that he needed to tread carefully with such a big name to make sure he stayed out of the press, out of jail. But Dylan knew that if Brooke had been threatened, his brother would do whatever he could to avenge her...and protect her.

Rafe gave him the name of Richard Bentley's hotel and the suite number.

* * *

Dylan knocked on Bentley's door hard enough that he would have made a hole through the heavy wood if her ex hadn't opened it. One little crack was all he needed once the doorknob turned, and then Dylan was pushing in and slamming it closed behind him.

Fear immediately leaped into Bentley's eyes. Of course, by now Dylan had seen plenty of pictures of the guy, both in Rafe's report and online. But Richard Bentley had been smug and totally in control in all of those images. Now, there was naked fear on his face.

"Who the hell are you? What are you doing?"

Dylan slammed his fist into the guy's jaw, enjoying the crunch of bone on bone.

That one hard punch was enough to have the guy begging. "Take my money. My wallet's by the TV. Take whatever you want, anything from my luggage, from the room."

With anyone else, the pathetic begging might have stopped Dylan from doing more violence. But what this guy and his family had done deserved more than one punch. Richard needed to feel enough pain, and enough fear, that he would never dare come near Grace or Mason again.

Dylan slammed his fist into her ex's gut. "I'm only going to tell you this once, so you'd better pay attention. Stay the hell away from Grace and her son. Forever."

The guy's eyes got big. "You're a Sullivan. The one she's fu—"

Dylan's hands were around the guy's throat before he could finish the word. "She told me what happened. Everything that happened, everything you and your parents tried to get her to do. I know she has it all on tape, every last word those sick people said to her. If you try to force her up against the wall to try to get at a kid who isn't yours in any way, you're going to pay."

The guy was gasping, wheezing now, but Dylan didn't want him to pass out. Not yet. Not until he heard every word.

"I know you think you're powerful. I know you and your family have probably won every legal battle you've ever been in. Between her word against yours and your parents', you probably think you could win because of your track record with charity. Even after hearing what she has on you, you might still be cocky enough to think you'll win. But Grace and her son, they're with me now. With my family. And if I were you, I wouldn't make the mistake of taking on a Sullivan. We'll tear you apart so fast and break you into so many pieces that your family will never recover."

Dylan had to force himself to drop his hands from around the guy's neck before bones were crushed. The bastard dropped to the ground, clutching his throat with both hands as he tried to choke down oxygen.

"Jesus, you're crazy." Her ex could barely scratch the words out. "You could have killed me."

"You haven't even seen crazy yet," Dylan said in an ominous tone, even as he smiled a joyless smile, one full of the promise of more pain than the guy could imagine even after nearly being crushed beneath Dylan's hands. "If I ever hear that you've come near Grace or her son again, if you ever try to sneak contact with them, if you ever threaten them in any way at all, my family will hit yours from all sides. We will leave no stone unturned. We will drag up every dirty, messy, ugly thing you and your ancestors have done, personal and business, for the past hundred years. And we will make damned sure the entire goddamned world hears about it all."

The guy had scooted back from him by then, still on the floor, with his back against the wall. "We don't want anything do with them anymore. It was a mistake. All of it was a mistake. Coming here. Ever being with her in the first place."

"You could have had everything." Dylan had seen stupid before, but never on this scale. Money and power often took everything good and bad about people and amplified it—but whatever good there might have been in Richard Bentley had long been buried by the cocky belief that he could get away with anything because no one could touch him. "One misstep and I'll make sure you're left with absolutely nothing. Do you understand?"

"I won't speak to her," Richard said, his voice a whine of pain. "Won't do anything to her or the kid. I'll make sure my parents don't, either. We won't bother her again. Never again."

Dylan didn't trust the snake's words, but he trusted the fear he saw in his eyes, which said more than any spoken promises would have. He forced himself to rein in the rage still burning through him. Any more violence, however satisfying, would only take him down to her ex's level.

Without giving the worthless heap another look, Dylan left the building and headed for the harbor. He needed a fast, wild sail tonight to clear his mind and burn through his frustration, and most important of all, to figure out a way to win Grace and Mason forever.

CHAPTER TWENTY-EIGHT

"Grace, Mason, it's so wonderful to see you again!" Claudia Sullivan's smile was wide and genuinely happy as she opened her front door to let them inside on Sunday afternoon.

Dylan was so close to his mother that Grace figured Claudia would know what had happened yesterday. The whole horrible story, from thinking she was pregnant to Richard showing up, and then Grace pushing Dylan away. But Claudia's expression didn't show so much as a trace of anger.

"Thank you so much for watching Mason again," Grace said. "You've been so kind to help out while I've been working on the story about Dylan."

His name hitched in her throat, and she knew his mother must have heard it.

"I love spending time with Mason," Claudia said in a gentle voice. "But I also know how hard it can be to let go. And to trust someone else."

She could easily hear Claudia's message: *I know you've been hurt. And I agree that you have every right to be wary and cautious before trusting again.* There was no judgment, just understanding. And that's what made Grace feel even worse. Because even now, even after she'd pushed Dylan away, his family wasn't doing the same to her.

Again and again she'd told herself that only fairy tales worked like this—where the single mother of the baby meets the perfect guy with the perfect family and he falls head over heels for them both. She'd reminded herself just as many times that it had all happened too fast and had felt too good for the blaze of heat not to cool as quickly as it had ignited. But none of those painful truths meant she wanted to hurt Dylan or anyone in his family. Not when they'd all been so good to her and her son.

"Claudia, I need you to know..." She instinctively drew Mason closer, even though she knew he couldn't shield her heart and that she should never use her son for that purpose even if he could. "Dylan has been wonderful. He's been amazing with Mason. And if I could—"

Claudia stopped her impromptu and very painful speech by putting a warm hand over hers. "Go for your sail with my son. It will help make things more clear. I just know it will."

Repeatedly over the past two weeks, Dylan had said that sailing with him would give her the answers she needed to finally write a compelling magazine story about the heart of a sailor. But could it also give her the answers to her other questions about how to learn to trust—and love—again?

* * *

Dylan hadn't shaved and looked as though he hadn't slept, either. But he'd never looked more beautiful to Grace. Or more real and raw— as raw as she'd felt every second since she'd bolted her door behind him the day before.

She wanted to run to him, wanted to throw herself into his arms and never let go. Instead, she stood in the doorway of his boathouse and tried not to cry as she said, "Hi."

"Hi." Dylan studied her for a long moment. She could see that he was concerned about her—she hadn't been able to sleep last night, either—but all he said was, "I'm glad you're here."

She knew better than to try to say anything more than the two-letter word she'd barely managed without sobbing, so she simply nodded.

"I would have gotten the boat ready for us," he told her, "but I figured you'd want to be hands-on with as much as possible today."

Knowing she needed to pull herself together—and fast—she took a deep breath. "Yes, that would be great." The five extra words weren't much, but they were progress, at least.

Grace already knew most of the basic vocabulary of a sailboat from her research—*starboard* instead of *right, bow* instead of *front of the boat*—but within less than sixty seconds, she realized that learning about sailing from books or the Internet could never take the place of actual experience. And as Dylan talked her through performing a detailed visual check of the lines that raised and controlled the sails to make sure they weren't wrapped around each other; as he showed her how to make sure that they all had a figure-eight knot on the free end so they wouldn't pull through the pulleys or sheaves; as he taught her how to determine the direction of the wind by using the indicator at the top of the mast, she was glad to be able to sink into learning mode...rather than about-to-break-into-tears-at-any-moment mode.

Dylan talked her through maneuvering out of the harbor and into the Sound. There was a fresh breeze and a light chop, enough to make way at a fairly good clip. Grace didn't realize she was smiling until Dylan smiled back.

"It's good, isn't it?"

Her chest squeezed tight as she stared back at him—so tight that she actually couldn't breathe for a few seconds. "It's great."

You're great, was what she really wanted to tell him. *I'm sorry I pushed you away, but I had to. I have to be smart this time, have to be prepared for everything, instead of just being swept away again.*

But since she was here to learn to sail for her story, not to make things even worse between them, she said instead, "When you're on land all the time, even in a city with as much water around it as Seattle, you never realize just how amazing it is to actually *be* out on the water."

She loved the taste of the salt water on her lips. Loved seeing the billowing sails on the other boats around them on the Sound. There were powerboats and fishing vessels, too, but the sailboats were what caught her fancy and imagination.

As they scooted over the water and he showed her how to man the tiller, he said, "You're a natural. Just like I knew you'd be. How about we hoist the spinnaker so that you can see what this baby can do?"

Being out on the Sound with Dylan was already a rush, but just as she always wanted more when she was in his arms, now that she was in his sailboat, she wanted more speed, more spray flying over them, more of the rush that she could so easily become addicted to.

"Tell me what to do to get it up."

He smiled at her, a warm and appreciative smile that made her heart skip a beat or two. "We'll do it together."

The procedure to hoist the spinnaker didn't seem all that easy to Grace, but with Dylan patiently talking her through each step, they soon had the brightly colored third sail up, and then they really started to fly. So fast that she couldn't contain her laughter or the joy that bubbled up out of her regardless of all that she'd tried so hard to suppress since yesterday.

No wonder she'd read that the spinnaker was often called a *kite.* For a few beautiful minutes, she felt she was flying with it, billowing and unrestrained in the wind. She felt his hand on hers a beat before he spun her to face him.

"You love it," he said over the sound of the water crashing beneath the boat. "You love the speed. You love the thrill. And you're meant to love it, Grace. I've seen it in you from the start— it's why Mason loves learning new things, loves being pushed so high on the swings and racing his toy cars so fast. It's in your blood." With one hand on the tiller, he put the other on her shoulder to make her stay to hear him out, even as he had to raise his voice to be heard over the rising wind. "*I'm* in your blood. Just like you're in mine."

His mouth was on hers then, hard and hot and even more exciting than their speed as they flew over the water. She didn't know how long they kissed, but when the deck tilted beneath their feet, she thought at first that it must be from the way Dylan's kisses made her head spin and how desperately she wanted to never have to stop kissing him back. But when he suddenly pulled away, then looked out over the water and cursed, she realized the boat was tilting because the weather had turned.

Somewhere during their passionate kiss, the light breeze had shifted around to the north and became an extremely stiff wind. "We're starting to roll hard to leeward," Dylan called out to her as he guided the bow directly under the center seam of the spinnaker. For a moment, they seemed to teeter back to balance, but then another blast of wind knocked them over again.

He was still busy at the tiller when the spinnaker started to dip into the ocean, tilting and dragging the boat hard. Over the crashing waves and howling wind, she could just barely hear him yell, "We need to release the sheet to dump the water out of the sail, then lower the halyard on my cue!"

Dylan had talked about a sailor's instinct several times during their interviews, and now Grace knew exactly what it felt like to have instinct take over. She'd only read about this situation before and barely had enough experience to know how to sail on easy waters, but somehow her hands knew exactly how to release the spinnaker.

The moment the water was out and the sail had gone limp, Dylan was up gathering it and pulling the wet sail back into the boat. He called for her to release the halyard, and he pulled the spinnaker down from the mast.

For the next fifteen minutes, they sailed fast back toward the harbor, trying to outrun the dangerous storm that had come from absolutely nowhere. In just the same way, Grace thought, that Dylan had come into her and Mason's lives from out of the blue—dangerously sexy and addictive...and exactly what they'd needed to shake them out of their safe little rut, too.

CHAPTER TWENTY-NINE

"Jesus, Grace." They were still some way out of the harbor when the winds died down as suddenly as they'd come up. Floating easily again now, Dylan finally moved away from the tiller and put his hands on either side of her face. "I've never seen the wind whip up so fast on the Sound. I never would have taken you out into this kind of swell for your first sail if I had known. I planned to woo you today on my boat, to show you that I could be everything you needed me to be—but then I couldn't stop kissing you, couldn't keep from getting too lost in you even to notice the weather changing." With deep concern, his eyes moved over her face. "Are you okay?"

Maybe she should have been shaky. Maybe anyone else would have hated the ocean, and sailboats, after this. But Grace felt more alive than ever. And clearer, too, inside and out—as if the thick, hard waves of salt water crashing over the decks had washed her doubts, and her fears, away.

It was just as Dylan had said during one of their interviews: It was right when you were trying to hold everything tightly under control that the wind and waves decided it was high time to show you not only how vulnerable you really were, but also how precious every single moment was.

But it was more than just the ocean and its breathtaking power that had changed her. Grace and Dylan had been a perfect team when those winds had kicked up and tried to topple them over. And it hadn't mattered how long they'd known each other—or how long they hadn't—because when push came to shove, there was no one she would rather have had beside her to face the storm.

"I love you."

His hands stilled on her arms where he'd been running them over her to make sure that she wasn't hurt. "Grace?"

"I love you," she said again, already planning to say it to Dylan at least a million times over the next seventy years. "I love you so much, have loved you from the first moment you held Mason in your arms, but I was afraid to tell you. Afraid to even let myself feel that love, because I thought the only way to keep myself and Mason safe from potential danger was to be cautious. To keep my guard up. To think everything through from every possible angle.

And to always stay in control." She slid her hands through his soaking wet hair, sending salt water flying. "But you were right that going sailing with you would make everything clear. So incredibly clear that I can finally see that I'll never be able to control everything. I'll never be able to stop nature from rearing up, I'll never be able to stop the waves from crashing on the shore, and I wouldn't ever want to. Wouldn't ever want to turn my back again on what truly matters just so that I can stay in a holding pattern that feels safer. And I don't ever want to try to stop what I feel for you again, or settle for anything less than the truest love because risking my heart seems too frightening. Can you forgive me for hurting you?"

"I would forgive you anything, Grace. But there's nothing to forgive. Yesterday all your biggest fears came crashing down on you at once. Anyone would have reacted the way you did. Anyone would have needed breathing room."

"I hadn't thought I'd let the Bentleys make me feel like I wasn't good enough. But now I'm realizing that the way they treated me when they learned I was pregnant spoke straight to all the fears I hadn't wanted to admit to over the years."

"Everyone has the same fear that we're not enough."

"You don't."

He smiled, one of his beautiful smiles that always made her stomach flip-flop. "I have three older brothers who pretty much rule the world between them. And what they can't do, my cousins can. Sometimes I think the real reason I picked up sailing was because it was all that was left. I should have built my family a boat before now, but I couldn't. Because it turns out that I needed thirty years to realize that I could share my love of sailing with all of them without giving up who I am and what makes me special."

Did he have any idea how much it moved her to hear him admit to being scared, too? And that he wasn't afraid to show her his flaws? The Bentleys were so utterly consumed with being and looking perfect that they were also utterly inauthentic. Whereas life—real life the way the Sullivans lived it—was beautiful and wondrous...and sometimes messy and raw.

"I don't know what the future holds," she said. "I don't know if I'm supposed to be this much in love with anyone, or give up this much control. I don't know if something will happen to you on a boat one day, if you'll sail away and another storm will take you away from me. But I'm not going to let that stop me from asking you to marry me. Be my husband. Be Mason's father. And let us give you all of our love. *Forever.*"

She'd expected him to look at least as surprised by her marriage proposal as he had when she'd told him she loved him, but there wasn't room on his face for anything but pure joy.

"There's nothing I want more than to marry you and be Mason's dad." He drew her against him, and his mouth was nearly on hers when he amended that to, "Actually, there *is* one more thing I want."

But she already knew what it was, could read his mind now that the storm had passed just as well as she'd been able to read it when the waves had been crashing over them. "Let's start today, Dylan. Let's grow our family right here. Let's give Mason a brother or sister right now."

As quickly as they could, they steered the boat into the lee of an island, tossed the anchor, then stripped each other's wet clothes off. Gently, he laid her down on the wooden decking, warm and drying now from the sunshine that had emerged as soon as the storm had blown away.

"You're so beautiful," he said as he stared down at her. "I've fantasized about making love with you on my boat a million times."

The air was cool, but Dylan's warm hands and lips against her skin heated her up all over. "Even making love with you a million times," she whispered against his lips as he came into her and she wrapped herself all around him, "wouldn't be enough for me."

"I'll never get enough of loving you, Grace."

And...*oh my*...did she ever love how he loved her.

* * *

The next afternoon, Grace was so immersed in her writing that she didn't realize Dylan had walked into her living room carrying Mason until they were right beside her.

"Hi!" She lifted her lips to Mason's for a smooch and was very pleased to end up with one from Dylan, too. "How was the park?"

"We had an awesome time." Dylan looked down at Mason. "Didn't we?"

Mason answered in the affirmative with a cute little high five, then squirmed to get down to play with his toy cars.

"Looks like you're on a roll with your writing." He moved behind her to massage her shoulders, and it felt *amazing.*

"I am," she confirmed. "Finally."

"Do you need me to take Mason back out so that you can have more quiet?"

"No." It was the last thing she wanted. "I want you to stay."

They smiled at each other, both of them knowing just how much the word *stay* really meant. His request for her to stay for Mia and Ford's wedding at his parents' house and then her request for him to stay that night with her for the first time a week later had been their first important steps toward forever.

All along, as she'd worked on this cover story, she'd thought she needed to hide her feelings for Dylan. She hadn't been ready for anyone to see how much she loved him, because she hadn't been ready to admit it to herself yet, either.

But the truth was that everything she knew about the heart of a sailor had come from being loved by—and loving—him. So this cover story wasn't only about Dylan. It was about her, too.

Which meant that to create the most honest, most powerful piece of writing possible, she had to strip away all of the layers and lay her own heart bare.

She'd been utterly vulnerable on the sailboat during the storm and had come away feeling stronger and more hopeful than ever. And when she'd been vulnerable with Dylan, she'd come away with more love than she'd ever dreamed of. Now, she was just as vulnerable on the page while she wrote her love story for the man, the ocean, and the sailboats that had done so much to shape him—and she was finally loving every single word she wrote.

And every single moment with her beautiful sailor, too.

EPILOGUE

Two weeks later...

Adam Sullivan raised his glass of champagne for a toast to celebrate the marriage vows Dylan and Grace had just shared. They were in Dylan's boathouse—empty now as he got ready to begin his new commission for a custom thirty-eight-foot sailboat—and the sun was shining down on them all through the open panels on the roof. When Adam had designed the boathouse for his brother, he'd never envisioned a wedding taking place in the space, but it had worked out great, with more than enough room for family and close friends to witness their vows and have a little party afterward.

Dylan and Grace held Mason together as the three of them smiled for Mia, who was taking pictures as their unofficial wedding photographer. A short while later, when it was time for everyone to wave the three of them off on their sailing honeymoon to Cabo San Lucas in Mexico, Adam—and everyone else—was surprised to see the brand-new sailboat tied up to the dock just outside the boathouse.

Adam knew something was up even before his brother said, "It was a perfect day to marry the love of my life in front of the people who mean the most to us." Dylan paused to kiss both Grace and Mason, both of whom he was holding close. "And it's also the perfect day for us to give you all this boat."

Mia shot Adam an incredulous look before turning back to Dylan. "Are you saying that you made this amazing sailboat for *us?*"

Dylan wasn't able to do more than grin and nod before Mia was launching herself into his arms. Within seconds, Brooke and Tatiana and his mom were there—with all the men in the family soon joining in on the big Sullivan group hug, too. Little Mason was in his element, whooping it up with the big family that had so happily adopted him from that first Friday night dinner.

Everyone was on cloud nine, and Adam was extremely happy for them all. Only Dylan would make a killer sailboat like this to give away to his family. They were a lucky bunch. Adam had always appreciated that.

The only thing he *didn't* love just then was being the last single Sullivan in Seattle. Because if he knew anything about his family—and he could usually read each of them like an open book—they wouldn't rest until they'd seen him happily paired off, too.

After everyone had taken some time to admire their brand-new sailboat, Rafe intercepted Adam as he headed back into the boathouse to flirt with a pretty woman in a short black skirt who was serving champagne and hors d'oeuvres.

"You're a dog," Rafe said. "You know that, right?"

Adam barked once, making Rafe laugh.

"What's your schedule like Wednesday afternoon?" Rafe asked.

"I can open it up if you need me to." That was an easy one for Adam. Family always came first. "What's up?"

"Brooke needs to be at the lake to make extra truffle deliveries this week to some new accounts, and I've got a big case I need to head to Portland to wrap up, but we've got an appointment we really can't put off any longer."

"Who are you meeting with?"

"The wedding planner. And don't blame Brooke for this request," Rafe said as he lifted a hand to head Adam off at the pass. "When it turned out everyone else had a conflict on that day, she told me not to ask you and said she'd figure something out. But I know how heartbroken she'd be if we screwed things up with the wedding planner by canceling on her again because we haven't been able to coordinate our schedules lately."

Rafe knew just how to play it—Adam couldn't say no because he didn't want to do anything to hurt Brooke, either. "Sure, I can meet with the wedding planner."

"Thanks," Rafe said with a grin. "You're a life saver."

But something about Rafe's grin seemed a little *too* pleased. Clearly, thought Adam, the matchmaking by his family had already begun.

~ THE END ~

ABOUT THE AUTHOR

Having sold more than 4 million books, *New York Times* and *USA Today* bestselling author Bella Andre's novels have been #1 bestsellers around the world. Known for "sensual, empowered stories enveloped in heady romance" (Publishers Weekly), her books have been Cosmopolitan Magazine "Red Hot Reads" twice, have been translated into ten languages. Winner of the Award of Excellence, The Washington Post has called her "One of the top digital writers in America" and she has been featured by Entertainment Weekly, NPR, USA Today, Forbes, The Wall Street Journal, and most recently in TIME Magazine. She has given keynote speeches at publishing conferences from Copenhagen to Berlin to San Francisco, including a standing-room-only keynote at Book Expo America on her publishing success.

If not behind her computer, you can find her reading her favorite authors, hiking, swimming or laughing. Married with two children, Bella splits her time between the Northern California wine country and a 100 year old log cabin in the Adirondacks.

For a complete listing of books, as well as excerpts and contests, and to connect with Bella:

Visit Bella's website at:
www.BellaAndre.com

Follow Bella on twitter at:
http://www.twitter.com/bellaandre

Join Bella on Facebook at:
http://www.facebook.com/bellaandrefans

Sign up for Bella's newsletter at:
http://eepurl.com/eXj22

Manufactured by Amazon.ca
Acheson, AB